I0831564

MANमथ
NATH
दUTT

TRANSLATOR
EXTRAORDINAIRE

BIBEK
DEBROY

RUPA

Published by
Rupa Publications India Pvt. Ltd 2020
7/16, Ansari Road, Daryaganj
New Delhi 110002

Sales Centres:
Allahabad Bengaluru Chennai
Hyderabad Jaipur Kathmandu
Kolkata Mumbai

ISBN: 978-93-89967-01-2

First impression 2020

10 9 8 7 6 5 4 2 3 1

To

Gayatri (Iyer) and Makarand Paranjape

CONTENTS

PROLOGUE

Let me start on a personal note. I have been translating from Sanskrit to English for some time now.[1] How does one approach the task of translation? I tend to first look at the Sanskrit and do my own translation. I then compare my draft translation with what my predecessor translators have done, usually translators who have translated from Sanskrit to English, but sometimes, also translators who have translated from Sanskrit to so-called vernacular languages. At the time of translating the Bhagavad Gita in 2006, there were many other translators who had preceded me and I didn't notice Manmatha Nath Dutt as a predecessor. At the time of the Mahabharata translation, the predecessors were Kisari Mohan Ganguli and Manmatha Nath Dutt, with J.A.B. van Buitenen's University of Chicago translation also included.[2] I recognized that the Manmatha Nath Dutt translation existed, but I paid more attention to Ganguli and van Buitenen. Having read some chapters of the Dutt translation, I realized it drew heavily on Ganguli. After

[1] These translations have been (and will continue to be) published in the near future—Bhagavad Gita (2006), Mahabharata (2010–14/15), *Harivamsha* (2016), Valmiki Ramayana (2017), *Bhagavata Purana* (2018), *Markandeya Purana* (2019) and *Brahma Purana* (2020).

[2] This translation of the Mahabharata was never completed. I am deliberately refraining from providing complete references to the various translations mentioned in this paragraph, since those references are not directly relevant to this book. The ones that are relevant—K.M. Ganguli, F.E. Pargiter and H.H. Wilson—will be referenced later.

the Mahabharata, in 2016, I translated the *Harivamsha* and realized that Manmatha Nath Dutt was the only one who had translated it before me, at least in English. Not only did I use Dutt's translation for the purpose of comparison, I also became more aware of Manmatha Nath Dutt's existence. Who was this person? In 2017, I translated the Valmiki Ramayana. There were more translators for the Valmiki Ramayana than for the Mahabharata, and Manmatha Nath Dutt was one of them. Manmatha Nath Dutt and I are the only two people to have done unabridged translations, from Sanskrit to English, of the Mahabharata, *Harivamsha* and Valmiki Ramayana. Next, I tackled the *Bhagavata Purana* translation in 2018. There were other translators for this book as well, such as Bhaktivedanta Swami Prabhupada, Swami Tapasyananda and Ganesh Vasudeo Tagare, but Manmatha Nath Dutt featured in the list too. In 2019, I turned to the *Markandeya Purana* and my predecessor translators were F.E. Pargiter and Manmatha Nath Dutt. It was impossible to get away from Manmatha Nath Dutt. Whatever I wanted to do, he seemed to have worked on it earlier. As I was planning out the timeline for the Purana translations, I had decided that *Vishnu Purana* would be the next, after *Markandeya Purana*. However, the *Vishnu Purana* had been translated by H.H. Wilson and Manmatha Nath Dutt earlier. Consciously, to avoid Manmatha Nath Dutt, I changed the timeline and decided to do the *Brahma Purana* before the *Vishnu Purana*. Manmatha Nath Dutt had not translated the *Brahma Purana*.

Who was Manmatha Nath Dutt? It was as if his spectre started to haunt me. But almost nothing was known about the man behind the spectre, the man who had left his footprints in the sands of time for me to follow. As I started to dig, some facts tumbled out. Some of it was circumstantial evidence and quite a bit was speculation, though it was informed speculation. Except for a few bare bones that were hitherto known, the facts, the circumstantial evidence and the speculation are all new and are reported in the pages that follow. We learn about the man, and in the process, also learn about nineteenth-century Calcutta. I will take you down the leads I followed, some of which were false ones. But, those false leads are also necessary, so that we can eliminate some possibilities, and zero in on Manmatha Nath Dutt—the man and his work.

ONE

THREE AUTOBIOGRAPHIES AND A STORY

Sucheta Kriplani (1908–1974) was several things—freedom-fighter, member of the Constituent Assembly and the first woman chief minister of India. A lot has been written about her. Those biographical sketches typically start with her studying in Indraprastha College in Delhi. Aside of her being born into a Bengali Brahmo family in Ambala, there isn't much information available about her parents or grandparents. Sucheta Kriplani did write her autobiography, though she left it incomplete and titled it appropriately as *An Unfinished Autobiography*. It was published in 1978.[1] In it, she writes about her parents and grandparents. She was born in Ambala because her father, Dr Surendra Nath Mazumdar, was a medical officer in the Punjab Medical Service. She writes:

> My father, Surendra Nath Mazumdar, came from an old Brahmo family. My grandfather, Dinanath, born in a well-to-do zamindar family of Bengal, voluntarily left his home and embraced a life of hardship and poverty, though perhaps one of much spiritual

[1]Sucheta Kriplani, *An Unfinished Autobiography*, Navajivan Publishing House, Ahmedabad, 1978.

> and psychological satisfaction to him. As a young man on a visit to Calcutta, he attended a meeting of Keshab Chandra Sen, the leader of the Brahmo Samaj, purely out of fun and curiosity. But the eloquence of Keshab Chandra so moved him that, then and there, he decided not only to be initiated into the Brahmo faith, but to dedicate his life to its propagation. Keshab Chandra had twelve close disciples or associates who organized the work of the Samaj and took its message to different parts of India. My grandfather Dinanath was one of them.

This was her father's side. On the maternal side, she writes:

> My maternal grandfather Manamathanatha[2] Dutt was a scholar both in Sanskrit and in English. He had his own flourishing publishing house. He translated into English the Ramayana, Mahabharata, Gita and other Sanskrit classics. In those days the Indian States often organized conferences of scholars and honoured them with titles and other rewards. My grandfather had been honoured on several such occasions. His eldest daughter, Prembala, was my mother.

After Surendra Nath Mazumdar's death, Sucheta Kriplani's mother eventually settled down in Santiniketan.[3] She writes of the time of her father's death: 'That year, none of our elder relatives cared to pay a visit to us except mother's youngest brother who was a barrister practising in Kuala Lumpur in distant Malaya.' As we will see later, Manmatha Nath Dutt probably died in 1912.[4] Since Sucheta Kriplani was born in 1908, whatever she gathered about him was almost certainly information gleaned from her mother, Prembala. We also

---

[2]He spelt his name as Manmatha Nath Dutt.

[3]Prembala Mazumdar was well known in Santiniketan circles as a good singer. Her name features in old issues of *Visva-Bharati News*, the university's bulletin.

[4]There may be some variations in the way Bengali names are written. Unless it is a quote, or a reference to what someone else has said, the spellings will be the customary ones. In cases of quotes, we have naturally not changed the way names are spelt.

have the reference to a maternal uncle who was a lawyer in Kuala Lumpur.

That first Sucheta Kriplani quote has a reference to Keshub Chandra Sen[5] (1838–1884). Prosanto Kumar Sen (1874–1950) was the son of Prasanna Kumar Sen, and both father and son identified with Keshub Chandra Sen and the Keshub Chandra Sen side of the Brahmo Samaj movement, after the schism in the Brahmo Samaj. Prosanto Kumar Sen was a lawyer, a judge and several other things, and his books on criminal law and monopolies are read even today. Sushama Sen was Prosanto Kumar Sen's wife. She was both a social worker and parliamentarian. Her autobiography tells us that Prosanto Kumar Sen's sister, Charubala, was married to Manmatha Nath Dutt.[6] A reference to Manmatha Nath Dutt can be found in Sushama Sen's autobiography. She writes:

> Prosanto's elder sister Charubala was married to Manmathanath Dutt. She died at childbirth leaving her daughter Prembala (Noni), and her two infant sons. 'Noni' was a great pet of Prosanto's mother, she was also taken in charge by her grandmother (Didima). Later all the girls were happily married after our marriage.

Thus, we now have a name for Sucheta Kriplani's maternal grandmother. She was Charubala, Prembala's mother, Manmatha Nath Dutt's wife and Sushama Sen's sister-in-law. Charubala died in childbirth, leaving behind a daughter (Prembala) and two infant sons. Of these, the younger son would go on to become a lawyer in Kuala Lumpur. Sivanath Sastri (1847–1919) was an author, historian, educationist, social reformer and much more. Sivanath Sastri wrote a history of the Brahmo Samaj, and here is a quote from the second volume:

---

[5] He usually spelt his name this way.

[6] Sushama Sen, *Memoirs of an Octogenarian*, Anjali, Shimla, 1971.

> [...] the efforts of Bhai Prasanna Kumar Sen, formerly a member of the Apostolical Durbar, also require mention. Shortly after the death of his master, with the aid of his son-in-law, he established a higher class English School called Keshub Academy and carried it on for years till it has become a permanent institution.[7]

The master is a reference to Keshub Chandra Sen and the son-in-law is none other than Manmatha Nath Dutt, though Sivanath Sastri did not mention the name.

Netaji Subhas Chandra Bose (b.1897) also left his autobiography incomplete.[8] Subhas Chandra Bose was the son of Prabhavati Dutt Bose and Janakinath Bose. In his unfinished autobiography, he wrote:

> My father was descended from the Boses of Mahinagar, while my mother, Prabhabati (or rather Prabhavati) belonged to the family of the Dutts of Hatkhola [...] As mentioned in the first chapter, my mother belonged to the family of the Dutts of Hatkhola, a northern quarter of Calcutta. In the early days of British rule, the Dutts were one of those families in Calcutta who attained a great deal of prominence by virtue of their wealth and their ability to adapt themselves to the new political order. As a consequence, they played a role among the neo-aristocracy of the day. My mother's grandfather, Kashi Nath Dutt, broke away from the family and moved to Baranagore, a small town about six miles to the north of Calcutta, built a palatial house for himself and settled down there. He was a very well-educated man, a voracious reader and a friend of the students. He held a high administrative post in the firm of

[7] Sivanath Sastri, *History of the Brahmo Samaj*, Vol. II, Brahmo Mission Press, Calcutta, 1912.

[8] Subhas Chandra Bose, *An Indian Pilgrim: An Unfinished Autobiography*, Netaji: Collected Works series, Vol. 1 (originally published by the Netaji Publication Society, 1948), Oxford University Press, New Delhi, 1997.

> Messrs Jardine, Skinner & Co., a British firm doing business in Calcutta. Both my mother's father, Ganganarayan Dutt, and grandfather had a reputation for being wise in selecting their sons-in-law.

On his mother's side, Subhas Chandra Bose was thus descended from the Hatkhola Duttas and his maternal grandfather was named Kashinath Dutta. There is a road named Kashinath Dutta Road in Kolkata and it is in Cossipore, in ward number one. Prior to the Hindu Widows' Remarriage Act of 1856, there was considerable debate, with petitions and counter-petitions. On 4 October 1855, a petition was submitted to the Legislative Council, supporting this legislation. This was led by Ishwarchandra Vidyasagar. However, other than Vidyasagar, the first person to sign it was Kashinath Dutta, from the Hatkhola Dutta family. This cannot but have been the same Kashinath Dutta.

The Hatkhola Duttas are an old zamindar family whose descendants trace the roots of the family tree—or at least some of its branches—far back in time, sometimes as early as the tenth century AD. At that time, the king of Bengal was Adisura. Historians have questioned this account, as have they the very existence of a king named Adisura. However, the belief is that King Adisura brought five brahmanas from Kanyakubja/Kannauj to Bengal. At that time, Purushottam Dutta also moved from Kanyakubja to Bengal, along with the brahmanas. For instance, according to a family account:

> Purushottam Dutta, our ancestor, settled down at a village called Bally which is currently a town in the Howrah district of South-West Bengal (Dakshin Rahra), on the bank of the Bhagirathi River [...] Purushottam's grandsons were Kanak Dutta and Nilambar Dutta. Nilambar stayed back in Bally, but, Kanak moved to a village known as 'Kadam Dandi' of West Midnapore in 11th century A.D.

Further down the line, there was Narayan Dutta.

> Murari Dutta, the great grandson of Narayan Dutta, had two sons—Ganapati Dutta and Tekari Dutta. The elder son, Ganapati, moved to a place called 'Halisahar'. The younger son, Tekari (12th in Purushottam's lineage) moved from Bally to Andul and established his residence in the 14th century. Tekari Dutta had inherited enough capital from his father to be able to acquire the extensive property of Muzzaffarpur Pargana, and become established as the first zamindar of Andul.

Andul is in Howrah and we have still not moved to Calcutta.

> In the 16th century, Kandarpa Ram Dutta Chaudhury inherited his father's zamindari. He had three sons—Ram Sharan, Gobinda Sharan and Hari Sharan, who were constantly at loggerheads with each other regarding the distribution of ancestral property. Gobinda Sharan Dutta Chaudhury severed ties with Andul, and went over to a place called 'Badar Rasa' somewhere in South Calcutta to establish his residence. It is believed that 'Badar Rasa' eventually expanded to become 'Gobindapur', named after Gobinda Sharan.

Gobindapur, Kalikata and Sutanuti were merged to form the city of Calcutta. Gobindapur was to the south, Kalikata was in the middle and Sutanuti was to the north. This naming after Gobinda Sharan varies with another account. According to this, four families of Basaks and one of Sheths founded Gobindapur, the village being named after the family deity, Gobindaji.[9]

Gobinda Sharan Dutta's grandson was Ramchandra Dutta, born around 1630. The East India Company wanted to build Fort William. Therefore, Ramchandra Dutta gave up some of the land

---

[9] This alternative account is given in H.E.A. Cotton's *Calcutta Old and New: A Historical and Descriptive Handbook to the City*, W. Newman and Company, Calcutta, 1907.

in Gobindapur and obtained land in Chitpur instead. The Ram Bagan area in Kolkata is named after Ramchandra Dutta, as is the market in Chitpur, which is known as Ram Bazar. Sushama Sen descended from the Rambagan Dutt family. But Chitpur was too noisy for Ramchandra Dutta. Without selling the Chitpur property, he moved to Hatkhola. Although many of them are referred to as the Hatkhola Duttas, strictly speaking, Hatkhola is the area around Nimtala Ghat Street, where there is a Dutta Para Lane in the region near Beadon Street. Ramchandra Dutta's grandson, Madan Mohan Dutta, had Madan Mohan Dutta Lane named after him and a famous puja is held there annually. Raja Binay Krishna Deb's book tells us, 'Madan Mohan Dutt, the son of Ram Krishna Dutt, lived at Nimtola in Sutanooti.'[10] There was/is a Dutta branch in the Chitpur/Baranagore area too and Kashinath Dutta Road is in Baranagore/Cossipore, where Kashinath Dutta built a large house. To complete the lineage story, Kashinath Dutta's father was Debi Prasad Dutta, Debi Prasad Dutta's father was Ramhari Dutta, Ramhari Dutta's father was Gorachand Dutta, and Gorachand Dutta's father was Ramchandra Dutta.

By the time Sushama Sen was born in 1887, that branch of the family had moved to 20 Beadon Street. After Sushama Sen married Prosanto Kumar Sen in 1904, they initially lived in 26 Beadon Street. There was a family association with the Beadon Street and we will return to this later.

Before moving away from Sushama Sen and her autobiography, let us bring in Romesh Chunder Dutt (1848–1909). Among several other things, Romesh Chunder Dutt translated, albeit abridged, the Ramayana and the Mahabharata into English. He was Sushama Sen's elder brother and, therefore, part of the Rambagan Dutt lineage. This means that he was Manmatha Nath Dutt's kin, if Manmatha Nath

---

[10] Raja Binaya Krishna Deb, *The Early History and Growth of Calcutta*, Romesh Chandra Ghosh, Calcutta, 1905.

Dutt was linked to the Hatkhola lineage. Romesh Chunder Dutt studied in Hare School. From Sushama Sen's autobiography, we also learn that Romesh Chunder Dutt's father was Ishan Chunder Dutt and Romesh Chunder Dutt's paternal uncle was Soshee Chunder Dutt, who died in 1885. Romesh Chunder Dutt's elder brother was Jogesh Chunder Dutt.

> On Ishan Chunder's death, his brother Soshee Chunder became the guardian of his nephews and nieces. Soshee Dutt, also a distinguished scholar of Hindu College, won fame for his idiomatic English. Jogesh Chunder said of his uncle Shoshee Dutt: 'He too used to sit with us at nights, and our favorite study used to be pieces from the works of English poets.'[11]

At that time, the family lived in Maniktola Street, now known as Romesh Chunder Dutt Street. Ramesh Datta Street (the way it is spelt now) is very close to Beadon Street. I will talk about a road named after Manmatha Nath Dutt later. If you ask someone today about this road in Kolkata and after whom it is named, the inevitable answer will be—someone from the Hatkhola Dutta lineage. Since all the famous Duttas, including those after whom roads are named, were from the Hatkhola line, it is assumed that Manmatha Nath Dutt must have been from the same family. This is a false lead and red herring, but it is a very tempting red herring. As we will soon see, Manmatha Nath Dutt's parentage had nothing to do with Hatkhola.

Let us be a bit more accurate. Let us call our Manmatha Nath Dutt—Manmatha Nath Dutt (W), 'W' for writer. Manmatha Nath Dutt (W)'s parentage had nothing to do with Hatkhola. But there was another Manmatha Nath Dutt too and he was Manmatha Nath Dutt (D)—'D' standing for doctor. Manmatha Nath Dutt (D) was from the Hatkhola lineage and he was Manmatha Nath Dutt (W)'s contemporary.

---

[11] Sen, *Memoirs of an Octogenarian*.

Through the lens of Western medicine, who was India's—and indeed, Asia's—first female physician? This is a standard general knowledge question and the answer is Kadambini Ganguly (1861–1923), born Kadambini Basu. She and Chandramukhi Basu were the first female graduates not only in India, but in the entire British Empire. In 1886, after graduation, Kadambini Ganguly obtained a medical degree from Calcutta Medical College. She was one of the first two female doctors. The other one was Anandibai Gopalrao Joshi, who studied for her medical degree in the United States. But just a few years earlier, there was Biraj Mohini Mitra, born in 1860. Biraj Mohini Mitra was married to a doctor named Manmatha Nath Dutt, from the Hatkhola lineage. This was Manmatha Nath Dutt (D). Biraj Mohini Mitra's father, Neel Kamal Mitra, sought permission that his daughter might be allowed to study medicine. However, at the time, there was no such provision for women.[12] That permission was only granted in 1883. Had that permission been granted, Biraj Mohini Mitra would have pipped Kadambini Ganguly by a year or so. Through Calcutta Medical College, Manmatha Nath Dutt (D) earned an LMS degree in 1878.[13] So the Calcutta University records tell us. Hence, Manmatha Nath Dutt (D) was just a few years older than Manmatha Nath Dutt (W).

There is a further complication. In Bengali, Jnanendra Kumar wrote a multi-volume collation titled *Vamsha Parichay*. This translates in English as description of lineages, and is essentially a description of the lineages of zamindars. Published in the closing decades of the nineteenth century to the first couple of decades of the twentieth, this collation is extremely difficult to get hold of. In the

---

[12] See the account in Chitra Deb's *Mahila Daktara: Bhinna Grahera Basinda* [in Bengali], Ananda Publishers, Kolkata, 1994. Also see, Sujata Mukherjee, 'Medical Education and the Emergence of Women Medics in Colonial Bengal', *Occasional Paper No. 37*, Institute of Development Studies, Kolkata, August 2012.

[13] LMS stands for Licentiate in Medicine and Surgery, and was a medical degree in vogue in British India. It existed concurrently with the Bachelor of Medicine (MB) degree. After Independence, the two were merged to form a unified MBBS degree.

seventeenth volume, there is a reference to Kashinath Dutta. We are told that he died at a relatively young age of 32 and that he was so generous that after he died, the citizens demanded a road in the locality be named Kashinath Dutta in his memory. The eleventh volume also mentions a Brahmo youth named Kashinath Dutta. It is certainly possible that there was more than one Kashinath Dutta. But it is much more plausible that the two Kashinath Duttas, both from the Hatkhola Dutta lineage, were the same. He is also known to be Subhas Chandra Bose's great grandfather, and the one who signed the petition on remarriage of widows. He is the one after whom the road was named. And since he was a Brahmo, if Manmatha Nath Dutt (W) was indeed descended from him, this is how Manmatha Nath Dutt came to marry into a Brahmo family and has that connection through Keshub Academy. In the Jnanendra Kumar collation, in the sixth volume, there is a stray reference to Manmatha Nath Dutt. We are told Manmatha Nath Dutt's son was Lalbihari Dutt and that Manmatha Nath Dutt was descended from the Hatkhola Dutt family. We are also told Lalbihari Dutt was Shibnarayan Basu's daughter's son. Therefore, Manmatha Nath Dutt was married to Shibnarayan Basu's daughter.[14] This bit of evidence, for what it is worth, suggests Manmatha Nath Dutt was a zamindar from the Hatkhola Dutta family. This cannot have been Manmatha Nath Dutt (D), who was married to Biraj Mohini Mitra. Neither can it be Manmatha Nath Dutt (W), the writer. Therefore, a third Manmatha Nath Dutt, Manmatha Nath Dutt (Z), enters the picture! This was Manmatha Nath Dutt, the zamindar, also a contemporary. In what follows, if used without qualification, Manmatha Nath Dutt

[14] Shibnarayan Basu was born in 1813 and died in 1861. Hence, for Manmatha Nath Dutt (W) to be married to Shibnarayan Basu's daughter, the age fit is less than perfect. But it is possible, since this would have been Manmatha Nath Dutt's second marriage, after Charubala's death. Though possible, this has a low degree of probability. Manmatha Nath Dutt (W) was born in 1865 and this woman, Shibnarayan Basu's daughter, would have been born around 1861, if not earlier.

will mean Manmatha Nath Dutt (W), our Manmatha Nath Dutt, the writer.

We will end this section with a short story or novella. When there is little information, some educated guesswork should be permissible. In all probability, Rabindranath Tagore knew Manmatha Nath Dutt. A bit on the numbers first. The Calcutta then and the Kolkata now differ in many ways. For a start, the population of Kolkata's urban agglomeration was more than 14 million according to the Census of India, 2011. Censuses are of recent vintage. A census for the town of Calcutta was held on 6 April 1876.[15] This gives us a total population of 4,29,535—4,09,036 for the town of Calcutta, 2,803 for Fort William and 17,696 for the port of Calcutta. In Manmatha Nath Dutt's growing up years, that was Calcutta's total population. As part of the 1901 census, there was a census of Calcutta town and its suburbs, in which Calcutta's population was 8,47,796. As in every census, literates and illiterates were counted separately. In 1901, the number of literates was 2,10,442. In Manmatha Nath Dutt's working years, his social and intellectual interactions would have been with a set of around 2,00,000 people. But, this is a gross overestimation. After all, the definition of literacy used in any census is very basic. There can be a better perspective though. But one has to make an assumption and it can hardly be called heroic. One has to assume that Manmatha Nath Dutt studied in Calcutta. Although it is possible that he studied somewhere else and moved to Calcutta subsequently, it is not very plausible. Hence, it is safe to assume he studied in Calcutta. However, by studying, I mean studying beyond school—his schooling could have been from anywhere, as indeed it was. The Education Commission tells us that in the period 1881–82, 356 students passed the First Arts (FA) examination of the University of Calcutta, 266 passed the Bachelor of Arts (BA) examination and 40 passed the

[15] Refer to <https://catalog.hathitrust.org/Record/100615605> (last accessed 2 January 2020).

Master of Arts (MA) examination. This is a far cry from the numbers we are used to now. From 1857 to 1881, 20,503 students passed the entrance examination of the University of Calcutta.[16] Of this, a total of 16,000 were Bengalis. By 1881, 1,494 Bengalis obtained the BA degree and 344 obtained the MA degree. Between 1881 and 1894, 11,340 Bengalis passed the entrance examination, 1,695 obtained the BA degree and 276 obtained the MA degree. Adding up the numbers, we get a cumulative total of 3,189 with BA degrees and 620 with MA degrees. Some with BA degrees naturally went on to study for the MA course. Therefore, there is a little bit of double counting in this. Nevertheless, we have a pool of about 3,000 people. That's the set Manmatha Nath Dutt would have interacted with, a size that is smaller than the membership aggregate of an average club. We aren't talking about 2,00,000 people. It is just about 3,000 instead. This meant it was a close-knit group, and everyone would have known everyone else—not even six degrees of separation required.

However, for the Tagore connection, there is more than the close-knit group argument. Rabindranath Tagore was born in 1861. Thus, he was roughly Manmatha Nath Dutt's contemporary. There is a 1964 film titled *Charulata*, directed by Satyajit Ray, which is based on a novella written by Tagore. In Bengali, the novella is titled *Nashtanida*, which translates to 'Broken Nest'. *Nashtanida* was written in 1901. Bhupati, one of the central characters, has independent means and does not need to work. He is interested in politics and the freedom movement and publishes a newspaper/magazine in English. His young wife, Charu, is neglected, though Bhupati does love her. Bhupati's brother-in-law, Umapati, is a lawyer[17], one who is not too successful. It is Umapati who encourages Bhupati

[16] These numbers and the subsequent ones are from Rochona Majumdar, *Marriage and Modernity: Family Values in Colonial Bengal*, Duke University Press, Durham, N.C., 2009.

[17] Note that Manmatha Nath Dutt's brother-in-law was a lawyer.

to start the magazine and helps him run the magazine and the associated printing press. Since Charu is lonely and bored, Umapati's wife, Mandakini, moves in as her companion. But she is too crass for Charu. Bhupati's cousin, Amal, studies in college and drops in often. A close relationship develops between Amal and Charu. Amal is a writer and also encourages Charu to write. Eventually, when Amal thinks the attachment has gone too far, he leaves with the intention to study in England. Charu is shattered. Realizing the close relationship that had developed between Amal and Charu, Bhupati too is devastated. The nest is broken. This is the gist of the story.

Let's now turn to the relationship between Charu and Amal:

> Charu, befuddled, came up to the end of the inner apartments of the house and clapped a number of times to draw his attention, but nobody seemed to listen. Angered, frustrated, she tried to concentrate on a book written by Manmatha Dutta in her verandah [...] Manmatha Dutta was a new author, whose style of writing was somewhat akin to Amal's, therefore Amal consciously refrained from praising him, reading out instead some excerpts of his books to his sister-in-law with enough mockery in his voice. Charu, irritated, would snatch that book from him and throw it away in disdain [...] Amal entered the verandah, and Charu pretended to read on, unnoticing, indifferent. Amal asked, 'What are you reading so raptly?' Watching her silence for some time, Amal lifted his head to her back, trying to read the name. 'Manmatha Dutta's *Galaganda*' (Goiter)!' he mocked.

Non-Bengalis may not have read the novella, Bengalis will have. But, how many people notice the name Manmatha Dutta when they read it? This is fiction and fiction need have no resemblance to reality. However, the depicted relationship between Amal and his sister-in-law is often asserted to have a basis in the relationship between Rabindranath Tagore and his sister-in-law. Autobiographical elements creep in, sometimes through the subconscious. If this logic is accepted for the relationship between Tagore and his sister-in-law, why should Manmatha Dutta not have been a real person? What was Charu's full name? Most people will say Charulata, which is why the film has that name. That's true. But if one reads the novella (in Bengali) carefully, one will find Tagore was a bit inconsistent in naming. Umapati is also Umapada and Charulata is also Charubala and to refresh our memory, Manmatha Nath Dutt's wife was named Charubala.

How many Manmatha Nath Duttas from the Hatkhola family were floating around? Was Manmatha Nath Dutt (W) also from Hatkhola? In that event, he was probably the Bhupati in Tagore's novella.

Since it doesn't make sense to quote from the Bengali edition, I will quote bits from Lopamudra Banerjee's translation.[18] This is how the novella begins.

> Bhupati had inherited a lot of money and generous ancestral property, so it was quite natural if he didn't bother to work at all [...] He had founded an elite English newspaper and that was how he decided to cope with the boredom that his riches and time, which was endlessly at his disposal, brought to him.

According to Subhas Chandra Bose's autobiography,[19] Kashinath Dutta's son was Ganga Narayana Dutta. There is a Ganga Narayana Dutta Lane in the Beadon Street area. Ganga Narayana Dutta is said to have had two sisters and one brother, Gyanendra Nath Dutta. Might it be the case that the count is incomplete? As unsubstantiated speculation, might it be the case that Manmatha Nath Dutt (W) was Kashinath Dutta's son? Might it be the case that father and

---

[18] *The Broken Home and Other Stories*, translated by Lopamudra Banerjee, Authorspress, New Delhi, 2017. This has translations of two novellas and six short stories written by Tagore.

[19] Bose, *An Indian Pilgrim*.

son had roads named after each other in close proximity? Or, was Manmatha Nath Dutt Ganga Narayana Dutta's son, with that count being incomplete? The timelines fit for either possibility. The Dutta family and its descendants were all over the place in Calcutta and many localities and roads were named after them. The surname Dutta is spelt in different ways in English. However, for Manmatha Nath Dutt, let's stick to the way he spelt it. Though descendants have traced branches of the family tree, some branches have still been left dangling, and the tree isn't complete. Manmatha Nath Dutt could be part of one of those missing links.

Though there was indeed a close-knit group of around 3,000 people, given the interests of both Rabindranath Tagore and Manmatha Nath Dutt, it is unlikely that their paths would have crossed, unless they actually met. There was no particular reason for Rabindranath Tagore to read what Manmatha Nath Dutt had written. However, it was also perfectly possible for them to have known each other, and the Brahmo Samaj connection makes this possibility stronger. One must remember the year when Tagore wrote the novella, *Nashtanida*—it was 1901. Rabindranath Tagore's grandfather, Dwarkanath Tagore (1794–1846), was a zamindar with several estates in what is now Bangladesh and after Debendranath Tagore's death, Rabindranath Tagore had to manage these. The estates in the eastern part of Bengal were in several districts. One of these districts was Pabna. Let us park this information. There will be a Manmatha Nath Dutt angle to Pabna as well.

TWO

THE CORPUS OF WORK

We know almost nothing about Manmatha Nath Dutt, not even about the amazingly productive 21-year period from 1891 to 1912. There is a piece written by Shashi Shekhar in the *Daily Pioneer* in 2011[20] and a German website with some information[21]. That's about it. We can speculate that he died in 1912, because the *Rig Veda Samhita* translation was left incomplete and ended abruptly. Shashi Shekhar drew on the German website too. Between Shashi Shekhar and the website, this is what we know about Manmatha Nath Dutt: (*i*) translator of Valmiki Ramayana, Mahabharata, *Harivamsha*, *Markandeya Purana*, *Agni Purana*, *Vishnu Purana*, *Garuda Purana*, *Bhagavata Purana*, *Mahanirvana Tantra*, *Manu Samhita*, *Parashara Samhita*, *Gautama Samhita* and *Kamandakiya Nitisara*; (*ii*) author of a book on Buddha; (*iii*) author of a book titled *Gleanings from the Indian Classics*; (*iv*) editor of a magazine called *The Wealth of India*; (*v*) rector of Keshub Academy; (*vi*) rector of Serampore College and (*vii*) MA, MRAS and Shastri.

---

[20] 'Genius Who Translated the Epics', *Daily Pioneer*, 7 November 2011. Available at <http://rec.arts.books.narkive.com/vFNlHfxW/the-genius-who-translated-hindu-epics> (last accessed 2 January 2020).

[21] Refer to <http://www.ramayana.pushpak.de/mndutt.html> (last accessed 2 January 2020).

This is accurate enough, though the list of books is incomplete and *Gleanings from the Indian Classics* had three volumes, not one. But, the bit about him being the rector of Serampore College is plain wrong. Manmatha Nath Dutt never described himself in that fashion. Nor is there anything to indicate any kind of association with Serampore College, an institution that was set up in 1818 by English missionaries,[22] with an original charter from the King of Denmark. It has a theological college and a non-theological college that, since 1857, has been affiliated with the University of Calcutta. A rector is a principal and Manmatha Nath Dutt's name does not figure on the list of principals of Serampore College. Nor was there any reason for him to be identified with an institution like Serampore College.

I believe that the following list of books and monographs which were authored or edited by Manmatha Nath Dutt is exhaustive. There are however two books that are not included in this list. I will return to those two later.

- *The Ramayana,* Girish Chandra Chackravarti, Deva Press, 65/2 Beadon Street, 1891. (The first six *kandas* were published in 1891.)
- *Gleanings from the Indian Classics, Tales of Ind,* Deva Press, 65/2 Beadon Street, 1893.
- *The Ramayana, Uttarakandam,* H.C. Das,[23] Elysium Press, 65/2 Beadon Street, 1894.
- *A Prose English Translation of Gita, or the Teachings of Srikrishna on the Field of Kurukshetra,* D.D. Bose, 46, Brojo Nath Mitter's Lane, Jhamapooker, 1895.
- *Srimadbhagavatam, A Prose English Translation,* H.C. Dass, Elysium Press, 65/2 Beadon Street, 1896.
- *A Prose English Translation of the Mahabharata (translated literally from*

[22] Especially, William Carey, Joshua Marshman and William Ward.

[23] We know from the records that H.C. Das was the printer and that his full name was Hari Charan Das.

the original Sanskrit text), H.C. Dass, Elysium Press, 65/2 Beadon Street, 1895–1897, 1901–05.[24]

- *A Prose, English Translation of Vishnupuranam (Based on Professor H.H. Wilson's translation)*, H.C. Dass, Elysium Press, 65/2 Beadon Street, 1896.
- *Kamandakiya Nitisara or the Elements of Polity*, H.C. Dass, Elysium Press, 65/2 Beadon Street, 1896.
- *A Prose English Translation of Markandeya Puranam,* H.C. Dass, Elysium Press, 65/2 Beadon Street, 1896.
- *Gleanings from the Indian Classics, Vol. II, Heroines of Ind*, H.C. Dass, Elysium Press, 65/2 Beadon Street, 1897.
- *A Prose English Translation of Hari Vamsha*, H.C. Dass, Elysium Press, 65/2 Beadon Street, 1897.
- *Vedas*, Society for the Resuscitation of Indian Literature and H.C. Dass, Elysium Press, 65/2 Beadon Street, 1897.[25]
- *Gleanings from the Indian Classics, Vol. III, Prophets of Ind*, R.K. Bhatta, Elysium Press, 65/2 Beadon Street, 1899.
- *Ayurveda or the Hindu System of Medical Science*, Society for the Resuscitation of Indian Literature and H.C. Dass, Elysium Press, 65/2 Beadon Street, Calcutta, 1899.[26]
- *A Prose English Translation of Maha Nirvana Tantra*, H.C. Dass, 65/2 Beadon Street, 1900.
- *A Short Sketch of Posta Raj Family*, H.C. Dass and Elysium Press, 65/2 Beadon Street, 1900.

---

[24] Karna Parva (1901) suddenly has the name of Rash Mohun Sircar as a publisher, in addition to Elysium Press. The Elysium Press address changes to Kashi Ghoshe's Lane, Beadon Street, and is no longer 65/2 Beadon Street. From Sauptika Parva (1902), both Rash Mohun Sircar and Elysium Press continue to be publishers, but the addresses of both change to 40 Nayan Chand Dutt's street.

[25] I have included this because it is mentioned in the Home Department's 1897 report. I find no other indication that such a book was ever published. The society did publish Raja Ram Rammohun Roy's translation, but that was in 1903.

[26] This can only be ascribed to Manmatha Nath Dutt because of the style. The preface was left unsigned and no author was mentioned.

- *Buddha, His Life, His Teachings, His Order (Together with the History of Buddhism)*, Society for the Resuscitation of Indian Literature, Elysium Bower, Baranagore, 1901.
- *A Prose English Translation of Agni Puranam*, H.C. Das, Elysium Press, 40 Nayan Chand Dutt's Street, 1903.
- *Outlines of Hindu Metaphysics*, Society for the Resuscitation of Indian Literature and H.C. Dass, Elysium Press, both addresses given as 40 Nayan Chand Dutt's Street, 1904.
- *Domestic Duty*, Society for the Resuscitation of Indian Literature and H.C. Das, Elysium Press, both addresses given as 40 Nayan Chand Dutt's Street, 1905.
- *Harita Samhita, Original Text with a Literal Prose* English *Translation*, H.C. Das, Elysium Press, 40 Nayan Chand Dutt's Street, 1906.
- *Us'anas' Samhita, Original Text with a Literal Prose* English *Translation*, H.C. Dass, Elysium Press, 40 Nayan Chand Dutt's Street, 1906.
- *Angiras Samhita, Original Text with a Literal Prose* English *Translation*, H.C. Das, Elysium Press, 40 Nayan Chand Dutt's Street, 1906.
- *Yama Samhita, Original Text with a Literal Prose* English *Translation*, H.C. Das, Elysium Press, 40 Nayan Chand Dutt's Street, 1906.
- *The Upanishads*, the E. Roer translation, edited by Manmatha Nath Dutt, Society for the Resuscitation of Indian Literature, 1907.
- *Atri Samhita, Original Text with a Literal Prose* English *Translation*, H.C. Das, Elysium Press, 40 Nayan Chand Dutt's Street, 1907.
- *Samvarta Samhita, Original Text with a Literal Prose* English *Translation*, H.C. Das, Elysium Press, 40 Nayan Chand Dutt's Street, 1907.
- *Ka'tya'yana Samhita, Original Text with a Literal Prose* English *Translation*, H.C. Das, Elysium Press, 40 Nayan Chand Dutt's Street, 1907.
- *Vrihaspati Samhita, Original Text with a Literal Prose* English *Translation*, H.C. Das, Elysium Press, 40 Nayan Chand Dutt's Street, 1907.
- *Daksha Samhita, Original Text with a Literal Prose* English *Translation*,

H.C. Das, Elysium Press, 40 Nayan Chand Dutt's Street, 1907.

- *S'a'ta'pata Samhita, Original Text with a Literal Prose* English *Translation*, H.C. Das, Elysium Press, 40 Nayan Chand Dutt's Street, 1907.
- *Likhita Samhita, Original Text with a Literal Prose* English *Translation*, H.C. Das, Elysium Press, 40 Nayan Chand Dutt's Street, 1907.
- *Vyasa Samhita, Original Text with a Literal Prose* English *Translation*, H.C. Das, Elysium Press, 40 Nayan Chand Dutt's Street, 1907.
- *The Upanishads,* the E. Roer translation, edited for the Society for Resuscitation of Indian Literature and H.C. Das, Elysium Press, 40 Nayan Chand Dutt's Street, 1907.
- *Gautama Samhita, Original Text with a Literal Prose* English *Translation*, H.C. Das, Elysium Press, 3 Furiapukur Street, 1908.
- *Vasishtha Samhita, Original Text with a Literal Prose* English *Translation*, H.C. Das, Elysium Press, 3 Furiapukur Street, 1908.
- *A'pastamba Samhita, Original Text with a Literal Prose* English *Translation*, H.C. Dass, Elysium Press, 3 Furriapukur Street, 1908.
- *Vishnu Samhita, Original Text with a Literal Prose* English *Translation*, H.C. Dass, Elysium Press, 3 Furriapukur Street, 1908.
- *The Garuda Puranam*, Society for the Resuscitation of Indian Literature, 3 Furriapukur Street, 1908.
- *The Dharma S'astra Text*, Sanskrit texts of 16 *samhitas*, H.C. Dass, Elysium Press, 3 Furriapukur Street, 1908.
- *The Dharma Sa'stra or The Hindu Law Codes* English *Translation*, Vol. II, H.C. Dass, Elysium Press, 3 Furriapukur Street, 1908.
- *Manu Samhita*, H.C. Dass, Elysium Press, 3 Furriapukur Street and Society for the Resuscitation of Indian Literature, 1909.[27]
- *Vedanta Sara*, the Sadananda Yogindra translation, edited by Manmatha Nath Dutt, H.C. Dass, Elysium Press, 3 Furriapukur

[27] This does not explicitly say that this translation was done by Manmatha Nath Dutt. Instead, it mentions him as the founder of the society.

Street and Society for the Resuscitation of Indian Literature, 1909.

- *Manu Samhita English Translation*, Society for the Resuscitation of Indian Literature and H.C. Das, Elysium Press, both addresses given as 3 Furriapukur Street, 1909.
- *Rig Veda, Text with Sayana's Commentary and a Literal Prose* English *Translation*, Society for the Resuscitation of Indian Literature and H.C. Das, Elysium Press, both addresses given as 40 Nayan Chand Dutt's Street, 1906–1912.[28]

Of the two books not included in this list, one was a compilation of English poetry for students. The book was titled *A Poetical Reader*.[29] Although compiled by Manmatha Nath Dutt, its subject was completely different. This slim book had 89 pages and was priced at 8 annas. A total of 1,000 copies were printed in the first edition and the book was published on 20 March 1888, before Manmatha Nath Dutt embarked on his other major works, including his many translations. In this book, Manmatha Nath Dutt was described as 'Head Master, Keshub Academy', not 'Rector'.

The second book, *Bangali Meye* (Women of Bengal), is actually a novel in Bengali. It seems to be the only published piece Manmatha Nath Dutt wrote in Bengali and his only work of fiction. I have been unable to obtain a copy of the novel. It has vanished. However, we know that such a book was published because of a brief unsigned review that appeared in *Calcutta Review* in 1886 in the section on vernacular literature.[30] The anonymous reviewer was harsh.

---

[28] This abruptly ended at VIII.2.30. The Sanskrit text was included, with Sayana's commentary, and there was an English translation.

[29] Refer to <https://archive.org/details/in.ernet.dli.2015.68666/page/n127?q=Keshub+Academy> (last accessed 2 January 2020).

[30] *The Calcutta Review*, Number 82, January 1886. Manmatha Nath Dutt's novel was titled *Bangali Meye*. It was published by Bengal Publishing Company in the Bengali year 1291, that is, in 1885. The address for Bengal Publishing Company was given as 200 Cornwallis Street.

> We sincerely trust that Babu Manmatha Nath Datta will now see that he is not yet fit to be an author, and that he would be promoting his own and his country's interests best, if he be so good as to accept, in a kindly spirit, and to follow the advice which we have given to the author of *Chirasangini*. That advice we also give in a friendly spirit to all young writers of drama and fiction in Bengali.

Chirasangini was a novel by Purna Chandra Gupta, also published in 1885. *Chirasangini* and *Bangali Meye* were reviewed together. The advice was as follows:

> Boy authors are, however, numerous in this country, and that is why so large a portion of Bengali literature is so worthless and unsound. Boy authors are, moreover, a curse unto themselves, because early authorship makes boys uncommonly vain, and the overpowering feelings of self-importance and self-satisfaction which are begotten in the unformed minds of boys by authorship of any quality or degree, arrest the development of their good sense and prudential instincts in a manner which proves disastrous in their practical everyday life. The pride of authorship blinds Bengali boys to the poverty, and in many cases, even wretchedness of their families, and thus they neglect their domestic duties and make themselves and those whom they are bound to support, extremely miserable. Boy authorship should be, therefore, earnestly and strenuously discouraged.

Though the review was harsh, there must have been other reasons why Manmatha Nath Dutt never wrote anything else in Bengali. Nor did he ever again try his hand at fiction. But this Bengali novel does have a sequel; there was a revised and reprinted version of the novel, published later, in 1892. We will save this for later.

To return to the main corpus in the English language, this is an impressive list in any day and age, notwithstanding the last decades of the nineteenth century and the beginning of the twentieth. Before 1914, there was no copyright legislation in India.[31] Therefore, once printed, books and monographs were freely reprinted. That was the case with Manmatha Nath Dutt's books too. This is a list of the original publications, not reprints by other publishers. There is one such book that I have not included in the list. This is titled *Vrata, Sacred Vows and Traditional Fasts.*[32] It is ascribed to Manmatha Nath Dutt and there is an unsigned 'Introduction' as well. However, the style and the English are completely unlike Dutt's, though there is certainly a late nineteenth/early twentieth century flavour to it. That's not surprising, because this book is based on a volume written by Rai Bahadur B.A. Gupte, and has nothing to do with Manmatha Nath Dutt.[33] The 'Introduction' to the book is also by Rai Bahadur Gupte, who was a distinguished author in his own right and didn't need to disguise himself as Manmatha Nath Dutt. Evidently, we have forgotten Manmatha Nath Dutt, but there is still some brand recognition. Rai Bahadur Gupte is further removed from memory.

A few more words about this list are necessary. First, in these books and monographs, the production quality is not very good and there are several typos. For example, names such as H.C. Das/Dass, Furiapukur/Furriapukur or Nayan Chand Dutt/Noyan Chand Dutt are not always spelt consistently. Second, this is a chronological list of publications of books/monographs, and not necessarily the sequence in which the texts were translated, or the works written. Many of these were serialized in a magazine first and thereafter published as books. The Press and Registration of Books Act was passed in 1867 and after this piece of legislation, a copy of every book published had to be

[31] The present Copyright Act of 1957 was preceded by a Copyright Act of 1914. Before that, the applicability of copyright legislation was tenuous, though British legislation from 1911 existed. Stated simply, there was no copyright on his works.

[32] Manmatha Nath Dutt, *Vrata: Sacred Vows and Traditional Fasts*, Indigo Books, New Delhi, 2002.

[33] B.A. Gupte, *Hindu Holidays and Ceremonials, with Dissertations on Origin, Folklore and Symbols*, Thacker, Spink and Company, Calcutta, 1916.

delivered to the government. Thus, every year the Home Department produced reports on publications. According to the 1896 report:

> Babu Pratap Chandra Ray's translation[34] of the *Mahabharata* was finished and a new and cheap edition by Babu Manmatha Nath Dutt commenced during the year. Several parts of the series titled *The Wealth of India*, also by the latter author, giving English translations of the *Srimadbhagavata*, the *Markandeya Purana*, and the *Kamandaki Nitisara* [...] were received in the course of the year.[35]

We will return to the monthly *The Wealth of India* later. According to the 1897 report:

> The Hindu publications under this head[36] include among others Babu Manmatha Nath Dutt's translation of the Mahabharata, F.E. Pargiter's translation of the *Markandeya Purana* with annotations, and a dissertation on the *Vedas*, also by Babu Manmatha Nath Dutt. Babu Manmatha Nath Datta's book entitled *Vedas* presents in a small compass the results of the researches of Colebrooke and other European scholars on the subject of those sacred books, and gives an analysis of their contents with a short dissertation on the Vedic theology and the state of society in the Vedic age. Many of the theories and suggestions put forth in the course of the work on the authority of European scholars can be hardly accepted as conclusive by orthodox native scholars.

Third, the many Dharmashastra texts (*samhitas*) published between 1906 and 1908 are actually slim monographs. In contrast, the subsequent 1908 Dharmashastra volume is a compendium of 16

[34] This is the Ganguli translation.

[35] *Report on Publications Issued and Registered in the Several Provinces of British India During the Year 1896–1897*, Government Printing Press, Calcutta, 1898.

[36] The head of 'religion'.

samhitas published together in a single volume. In terms of size, they aren't comparable.

A few more words about the book on the Vedas, evidently published in 1897 and described by the report on publications as not 'conclusive'. The report also states that this was a dissertation authored by Manmatha Nath Dutt. Indeed, there seems to be no such book authored by Manmatha Nath Dutt. However, in 1903, the Society for the Resuscitation of Indian Literature published Raja Rammohun Roy's (1772–1833) translations of the Vedas and the Upanishads titled *Translation of Several Principal Books, Passages and Texts of the Veds, and of Some Controversial Works on Brahmunical Theology*.[37] Perhaps, the use of the word 'controversial' in the title led the authors of the report to deduce the conclusions were not 'conclusive', if the dissertation by Manmatha Nath Dutt and this book are identical. In any event, the primary author of this book was not Manmatha Nath Dutt, but Raja Rammohun Roy. In addition to the translations, there were several essays on Raja Rammohun Roy. While some of these essays were clearly marked reprints, there were also essays by N.N. Ghosh[38], Mohini Mohun Chatterjee[39], Sitanath Tattvabhushan (more on him later), Manmatha Nath Dutt, Bipin Chandra Pal[40] and Brajendra Nath Sil[41]. None of these were marked reprints and all were written in 1896. Since none of these were marked reprints, these fresh essays must have been written for a specific purpose. The book also says 'Memorial Edition'. In

[37] Raja Rammohun Roy, *Translation of Several Principal Books, Passages and Texts of the Veds, and of Some Controversial Works on Brahmunical Theology*, Society for Resuscitation of Indian Literature and H.C. Dass, Elysium Press, 1903.

[38] Nagendra Nath Ghosh (1854–1909), who wrote several books on law and history, also wrote a biography of Kristo Das Pal. In the main body of the text in this paragraph, the names are spelt the way they were spelt in the 1903 book. In the footnotes, we have used the spelling that is customary today.

[39] Mohini Mohun Chatterji (1858–1936) was a lawyer, scholar and theosophist.

[40] Bipin Chandra Pal (1858–1932) was a nationalist, freedom fighter and writer.

[41] Brajendra Nath Seal (1864–1938) was an author and philosopher.

1903, exactly 100 years after Raja Rammohun Roy's death, one can understand the use of the expression 'Memorial Edition'. But since the expression 'Memorial Edition' was used, there may well have been an edition earlier, perhaps in 1896 or 1897, since those fresh essays were authored in 1896. Hence, this could very well be the book the report mentioned. Typically, a special edition is brought out to commemorate the elapse of a certain number of years after an event, say 50, 60 or 75. A natural peg in 1897 was the 175th anniversary of Raja Rammohun Roy's birth. Perhaps that is when the book was first brought out, reprinted again in 1903.

In this collection, Manmatha Nath Dutt himself wrote on Raja Rammohun Roy as an educationist. Though the essay was on Raja Rammohun Roy's views, the manner in which Manmatha Nath Dutt wrote almost certainly indicates the views of the latter too.

> All right-thinking men in the country are at the present day sufficiently alive to the good that has been done to India by the introduction and spread of English education. India has glorious traditions—India has a splendid literature of her own. In India civilization dawned before other nations of the world came into being. All this is true no doubt; but England will always have the credit of rescuing her from a dreadful oblivion into which she fell before the advent of the English by the positive apathy and antipathies of the preceding eras [...] A keen interest in her literature, philosophy and ancient civilization is being gradually evinced by the leaders of thought in the West. This has been mainly brought about by the spread of English education in India, which has opened a means of communication between the natives of the soil and its foreign rulers and has become the key to unlock the portals of the grand intellectual treasures imbedded in the literature of Ancient India [...] It is not by merely placing a fruitful

> education scheme before the country that he advanced the educational cause of India, but he gave a practical proof of his views by taking a prominent part along with Sir Edward Hyde East and David Hare in the establishment of the Hindu College.

Hindu College, which was subsequently renamed Presidency College was established in 1817, and so, 1897 was the eightieth year of the setting up of the college.

Let us return to Manmatha Nath Dutt again. The corpus of his work that goes beyond mere editing has some distinct buckets: (*i*) translations of Bhagavad Gita, Ramayana, Mahabharata and *Harivamsha*; (*ii*) translations of the Puranas; (*iii*) translations of the Dharmashastra texts; (*iv*) incomplete translation of *Rig Veda*; (*v*) translation of *Mahanirvana Tantra*; (*vi*) retelling stories (*Gleanings from the Indian Classics*); (*vii*) books on Hinduism (on Ayurveda, metaphysics and domestic duty); (*viii*) a book on the Buddha and (*ix*) as an outlier, a monograph on the Posta Raj. I did a rough word count of the number of words Manmatha Nath Dutt wrote in these books, that is, the number of words he wrote himself, in the translations and in the introductions/prefaces, excluding the works of others. This is a rough word count and is by no means exact, and also because I calculated the average number of words in a typical Manmatha Nath Dutt page and multiplied it by the number of pages. I didn't exactly count the number of words in the entire corpus. The estimate is 2.6 million words. Since this was within the 21-year productive period of his life, from 1891 to 1912, the figure translates to around 1,24,000 words a year or 10,300 words a month—not a very easy track record to emulate in any age.

The Statesman newspaper was started in 1875 and soon after, there was a debate that attracted the attention of many educated people in Calcutta. This was triggered by Reverend William Hastie (1842–1903), who led quite a colourful life, replete with libel charges and imprisonment. But that came later. The time that we are talking about, was when he was the principal of the General Assembly's Institution, which would later be known as Scottish Church College. The controversy in the editorial pages of *The Statesman* lasted from 23 September 1882 to 14 November 1882. The trigger was a *shraddha* (funeral) ceremony held at the Shobhabazar Rajbari (palace). On the occasion of the *shraddha* ceremony, the family idol, Gopinathji, was placed on a silver throne. On 20 September 1882, *The Statesman* published a report on the funeral ceremony, at which, several notable people were present. This account infuriated William Hastie and he dashed off three letters to the newspaper, published on 23th, 26th and 29th of September 1882.[42] Reverend Hastie was livid at this example of idolatry and implicitly suggested that the only hope for Hindus was to become Christians. The third letter eventually provoked Bankim Chandra Chatterjee, who responded with a letter to the editorial pages on 6 October 1882. Since Bankim Chandra Chatterjee signed this letter as 'Ramchandra', it was not initially known that this was Bankim Chandra Chatterjee writing.[43] Hastie responded and more letters followed. Bankim Chandra Chatterjee never quite got into a futile debate with Hastie.

In that exchange of letters, what is relevant for us is Bankim Chandra Chatterjee's first letter, signed 'Ramchandra' and titled 'The Modern St Paul'. It should be quoted in its entirety.

> Sir, will you allow me to suggest to Mr. Hastie, who is so ambitious of earning distinction as a sort of Indian St. Paul, that it is fit that he should render himself better acquainted with the doctrines of the Hindoo religion before he seeks to

---

[42] All the six Hastie letters were subsequently published as *Hindu Idolatry and English Enlightenment: Six Letters Addressed to Educated Hindus Containing a Practical Discussion of Hinduism*, Thacker, Spink and Company, Calcutta, 1883.

[43] In the form of a book, these letters, and some others, were published much later, in 1940. Bankim Chandra Chatterji, *Letters on Hinduism* (edited by Brajendra Nath Banerji and Sajani Kanta Das), M.M. Bose, Calcutta, 1940.

demolish them? As matters stand with him, his arguments are simply contemptible; and I think the columns of *The Statesman* might have been more usefully occupied by advertisements about Doorga Puja holiday goods than by trash which renders the champion of Christianity contemptible in the eyes of idolaters. This may be harsh language, but the writer who mistakes Vedantism for Hinduism and goes to Mr. Monier Williams for an exposition of that doctrine, hardly deserves better treatment. Mr. Hastie's attempt to storm the 'inner citadel' of the Hindoo religion forcibly reminds us of another equally heroic achievement—that of the redoubted knight of La Mancha before the windmill. Let Mr. Hastie take my advice, and obtain some knowledge of Sanskrit scriptures in the ORIGINAL. Let him study then critically all the systems of Hindoo philosophy—the *Bhagabatgita*, the *Bhakti-Sutra* of Sandilya, and such other works. Let him not study them under European Scholars, for they cannot teach what they cannot understand; the blind cannot lead the blind. Let him study them with a Hindoo, with one who believes in them. And then, if he should still entertain his present inclination to enter on an apostolic career, let him hold forth at his pleasure, and if we do not promise to be convinced by him, we promise not to laugh at him. At present, arguments would be thrown away on him. There can be no controversy on a subject when one of them controversialists is in utter ignorance of the subject matter of the controversy; and if under such circumstances the 'Olympians only yawn' and do not assert, Mr. Hastie has only to thank his own precipitate ignorance.

This was in 1882. We will discover later that Manmatha Nath Dutt was born in 1865. Given Manmatha Nath Dutt's year of birth, he would have been 17 then, an impressionable age, and it is also fairly obvious which side of the debate he would have been on. The likes of Reverend Hastie weren't likely to learn Sanskrit and read the texts in the original. Hence, Manmatha Nath Dutt set out to do this in English. Here is a quote from the introductory section of *Gleanings from the Indian Classics*, Vol. I, published in 1893, 11 years after the Hastie versus Bankim Chandra exchange occurred.

> The Hindus and their Religion are the most misunderstood thing in the modern world. The civilized people of the Western World labour under the notion that the Hindus are a people a little better than the aborigines of Africa and their Religion is not better than the grossest form of idolatry [...] We do not exaggerate; so long as we cannot remove the notion that is predominant all over the Western World, we know we shall find none to agree with us in saying what we have just now said. This work is an attempt in that direction. This is an attempt to popularize the Hindu Literature, Philosophy and Religion among the Western nations. We are treading the footsteps of the great Rishis. We are following the examples and adopting the means of those great men, who made India what it is. We shall give their tales, their annals, legends and histories, their sweet verses and sweeter poems in popular and easy English, suiting modern tastes and Western methods. Hindu Literature, History, Philosophy and Religion are so extensive that it is not expected to be mastered in a day or explained in a book. This little work is the first step to give an idea of them, it will be followed by a series of works, in each and every one of which attempts will be made to popularize Hindu Literature, History, Philosophy and Religion.

There must also have been a Bankim Chandra Chatterjee influence through the monthly magazine, *Bangadarshan*. This was founded by Bankim Chandra Chatterjee in 1872 and he was the editor for four years. After a short gap of a year, Bankim Chandra Chatterjee's younger brothers, Sanjib Chandra Chattopadhyay (Chatterjee) and Srish Chandra Chattopadhyay, became the editors. From 1901, there was a new version of *Bangadarshan*. It is certain that Manmatha Nath Dutt read *Bangadarshan*, like every educated Bengali of the time.

At some point, Manmatha Nath Dutt must have received some kind of reprint permission from Heeralal Dhole. Strangely, as is the case with Manmatha Nath Dutt, not much is known about Heeralal Dhole either. Heeralal Dhole brought out the Dhole Vedanta Series. Lala Sreeram translated *Vicharsagar* and this was published by Heeralal Dhole in 1885.[44] This did not carry the Dhole Vedanta Series imprint. The *Vichar Mala* of Anatha Das, also translated by Lala Sreeram, was published in Dhole's Vedanta Series.[45] At the end of this book, there is a note, dated 1 January 1886, by Heeralal Dhole. The subject of the note is Dhole's Vedanta Series.[46] This tells us a bit about the Dholes, Nandalal and Heeralal. This series published the *Vedantasara* of Paramhansa Sadananda Jogindra. Heeralal Dhole's note quoted reviews of this volume. It says, 'The English rendering of it is from the erudite and scholarly pen of our friend Dr Nandalal Dhole, Late Surgeon to the Courts of Khetree and Marwar.' A different review of the same volume states:

> It is very ably prefaced by the Editor, Mr Heeralal Dhole whose learned and patriotic spirit longs to see the revival of the once glorious, spiritual or religious advancement of our Aryan nation. The Memoir and the English Translation of the Original Sanscrit Text by Dr Nandalal Dhole, late Surgeon to the Courts

---

[44] *The Metaphysics of the Upanishads: Vicharsagar*, translated with copious notes by Lala Sreeram (Heeralal Dhole, 127 Musjidbaree Street, 1885, printed by Nilambara Vidyaratna, Vedanta Press, Musjidbaree Street).

[45] *The Vichar Mala*, translated by Lala Sreeram, Dhole's Vedanta Series (Heeralal Dhole, 127 Musjid Baree Street, 1886, printed by Nilambara Vidyaratna, Vedanta Press, 56 Beadon Street).

[46] Typos and inferior production quality characterized this set of publications also. For example, January is typed Jaunary and the address is given as 127 Musjidbari Street.

> of Khetree and Marwar, with copious annotations do justice to his ripe erudition.

The note also announced the forthcoming translation of Vidyaranaswami's *Panchadasi*. The model followed was identical to the model followed in the Manmatha Nath Dutt translations—monthly instalments, culminating in an eventual book.

> This work is being issued in monthly parts. Annual subscription for the English Edition Rs. 6 in India; Rs. 7 in Ceylon, Straits Settlements, China Japan, ann [*sic*] Australia; 14 shillings in Africa, Europe, and U.S. America. Single copy Re. 1. Dr. Nundalal Dhole is in charge of the English Translation.

Panchadasi was published in Dhole's Vedanta series, but there was a difference. By the time it was published in two volumes in 1886, Nandalal Dhole was dead. The second edition, published in 1899, still bore the Dhole Vedanta Series imprint. However, the publisher was listed as Heeralal Dhole, Musjid Bari Street and Society for the Resuscitation of Indian Literature, 65/2 Beadon Street. The printer was H.C. Das of Elysium Press, 65/2 Beadon Street.[47] The preface to the first edition was by Nandalal Dhole. In the second edition, there was a footnote by Heeralal Dhole, and this read:

> And so it did happen that with this short Biographical Sketch of the author [meaning Vidyaranya Swami], the English translator of the Panchadasi paid his tribute of Nature. He died in his 47th year on the 14th of March, 1887 at 5-30 a. m., deeply regretted by all who knew him.

After Nandalal Dhole died, Vedanta Press, at least the one that

---

[47] *A Handbook of Hindu Pantheism: The Panchadasi of Sreemut Vidyaranya Swami*, translated with copious annotations by Nandalal Dhole (LMS, Heeralal Dhole, Society for Resuscitation of Indian Literature and Elysium Press, 1899). I have not been able to get copies of the first edition. By profession, Nandalal Dhole was a physician.

published Dhole's Vedanta Series, probably wound up. At any event, it does not seem to have ever published anything else. How did Heeralal Dhole and Manmatha Nath Dutt come into contact with each other? Heeralal Dhole's address in Masjid Bari Street and Manmatha Nath Dutt's address were not that far from each other, and Vedanta Press at 56 Beadon Street was even closer to 65/2 Beadon Street. What happened to Heeralal Dhole later? We don't know. He too seems to have vanished.

In the 1904 book on Hindu metaphysics, Manmatha Nath Dutt inserted a chapter on 'Maya', which is based on something Nandalal Dhole had written. There was a footnote to this chapter, which states:

> We glean this from a valuable contribution by Dr Nandalal Dhole, the eminent translator of the Panchadasi in the columns of *The Philosophic Inquirer*, Vol. VII, p. 73, and insert it here with the kind permission of his son, our esteemed friend and brother[48] Babu Heeralal Dhole.

But, the paths of Heeralal Dhole and Manmatha Nath Dutt were different. *Vedantasara* was published by Heeralal Dhole in 1883. The following is a quote from Heeralal Dhole's preface.

> The twice-born has retired from the conspicuous position of his ancestors behind the desk of a government office, or a merchant's counter, leaving the key to rust in the lock of Brahmanic lore, to be turned by the mighty hand of a Blavatsky and the patriotic and philanthropic erudition of an Olcott, till whipped into a sense of duty these 'bad Aryans' have returned in fealty and allegiance to the mother-country, and are now preparing in one grand effort to put the shoulder to the wheel [...] With successive generations the gulf grew wider, the thirst for service grew universal, and the quiet and engrossing study

[48] Though we should not read too much into this, 'brother' was how members of the Brahmo Samaj often addressed each other.

> of the Aryan Rishis, their sacred books and writings, came to a stand-still [...] The Ramayana and the Mahavarata were fabulous tales spun out into coarse yarns, without any redeeming feature; even the Vedas and Puranas were no better [...] At such a juncture the appearance of the two strangers amongst us—the indefatigable President-Founder and the illustrious and excellent Madame Blavatsky was an invaluable blessing.

These were the views of the Theosophical Society, and certainly not something Manmatha Nath Dutt would have subscribed to. Therefore, when Manmatha Nath Dutt reprinted *Vedantasara* in 1909, he had his own preface.

> Vedanta is not theology, because it denies the conception of an anthropomorphistic deity. It is not ethics alone, since in the later development of soul-existence, it denies the paradox of good and evil. It is not a science of things, since it proves things to be non-existent and illusory. It is a science whose exact English synonym is hard to find out, the Science of Seeing being the best translation.

Had one not used English expressions, the appropriate word is *darshana*, a word that is imperfectly captured in the realm of 'philosophy'.

We have a society, a magazine and a press. The *Manu Samhita* translation describes Manmatha Nath Dutt as the founder of the Society for the Resuscitation of Indian Literature. This society probably did not have any other office-bearers. The objectives of this society were stated in the *Ayurveda* monograph[49], and are as follows:

1. To undertake the publication of rare Sanskrit texts not published before.

[49] Manmatha Nath Dutt, *Ayurveda or the Hindu System of Medical Science*, Society for the Resuscitation of Indian Literature and H.C. Dass, Elysium Press, Calcutta, 1899.

2. To undertake the publication of cheap editions of texts already published.
3. To publish popular editions of works relating to the antiquity of Indian literature.
4. To publish such works of oriental scholars as have gone out of print.
5. To undertake translations of standard Sanskrit works into various living languages.

The address was 65/2 Beadon Street.

The insert also stated, 'Any donation or pecuniary help for the furtherance of the objects of the Society, will be thankfully received and acknowled [*sic*] the Secretary.'[50] That appeal about donations or pecuniary help was not repeated. Either it wasn't needed, or it didn't help.

The society had five different objectives and I wish to stress upon this point. Manmatha Nath Dutt is invariably described as a translator, from Sanskrit to English. Indeed, he was that. However, he was also an author under the head, 'To publish popular editions of works relating to the antiquity of Indian literature.' He seems to have received little acknowledgement for this. In fact, the negative references to his translations are almost exclusively due to what was said about his translation of the Mahabharata. Before Manmatha Nath Dutt, Kisari Mohan Ganguli published his translation of the Mahabharata. The Ganguli translation was funded and published by Pratap Chandra Roy. Thanks to Pratap Chandra Roy and his wife, we know something about Ganguli. P. Lal compiled an annotated Mahabharata bibliography in 1967, which provides quite a bit of information about Ganguli. However, P. Lal was rather dismissive about Dutt. This negative reference to the Dutt translation in this annotation may also have something to do with Dutt receiving less

---

[50] The text of the *Ayurveda* monograph also has several typos.

attention than he deserves.[51] In similar vein, Alf Hiltebeitel also put forth his opinion on the translations of the Mahabharata by both Ganguli and Dutt.

> The first, which I will focus on shortly, is the 1884–1896 translation by Kisari Mohan Ganguli, who labored anonymously, leaving the credit for the work to its patron, fund-raiser, publisher, and spokesman Pratap Chandra Roy. The second, by Manmatha Nath Dutt (1895–1905), did little more than shamelessly crib from the Ganguli–Roy translation. It changed nothing substantial, and, quite gratuitously, did no more than try to improve the English. Ganguli, Roy, and Dutt were all Bengalis, and we may place their work in the setting of the so-called Bengal Renaissance, which occurred while the capital of the British empire was still in Calcutta, that is, in Bengal.[52]

The charge of copying is a trifle unfair. As has just been mentioned, translations were only part of what Manmatha Nath Dutt did. There were indeed problems with the translations. First, the production quality was not the best and there were typos. Second, Manmatha Nath Dutt wasn't always original, deliberately so. His object was dissemination. The Ramayana translation was an exception, where

---

[51] P. Lal writes:

> This is the second complete translation, in three volumes, of the Mahabharata, by the Rector of Keshub Academy. It is the only one that gives a verse-by-verse rendering. Dutt follows the Kisari Mohan Ganguli version closely in many places, but is more prudish: Ganguli Latinises, Dutt omits. In Book I (*Adi Parva*), LXIII, 'slokas 50 to 52 not translated for obvious reasons' […] in the same book, CIV, slokas 14 to 20 are also 'not translated for obvious reasons'.

Taken from P. Lal, *An Annotated Mahabharata Bibliography*, Writers Workshop, Calcutta, 1967. In case one has missed the point, the Ganguli translation did not give specific verse (*shloka*) numbers. The Dutt translation had these verse numbers.

[52] Alf Hiltebeitel, 'Some Thoughts on Translating Translation from Korea to India'. Available at <https://www2.gwu.edu/~eall/archive/special/Alf_Hiltebeitel.htm> (last accessed 2 January 2020).

much more of Manmatha Nath Dutt comes through. In subsequent translations, introductions became rare and terse and he often drew on the work of others. For instance, though the language did change, the Dutt translation does draw a fair bit from the Ganguli translation. In 1896, much more than his Mahabharata translation drew on Ganguli, his *Vishnu Purana* translation drew on Horace Hayman Wilson's (1786–1860) translation of the same text,[53] and this was explicitly acknowledged in the sub-title itself. It was also explicitly acknowledged in the preface, where he says:

> In this translation ofVishnupuran I have principally drawn upon Professor H.H. Wilson's splendid work, and have tried, as best as lies in my power, to interpret the ancient thought entombed in this great work. My work is not so much intended for scholars as for the general readers who have not the time and leisure to read the original. Professor Wilson's book is very costly and cannot be always procured by the readers; and in the face of this difficulty I believe my edition will not be unwelcome to the general public.

Irrespective of whether copyright legislation existed or not, this was never plagiarization in the legal sense we use the word now. However, this tendency to disseminate the work of others probably meant that Manmatha Nath Dutt never quite got the credit he deserved, at least for the translations. There will be more on this issue in Chapter 5, where the argument will be reinforced by tapping a somewhat unsual source.

This was a period when serious translations were being done in Bengal. From 1895, Manmatha Nath Dutt started to describe himself as MRAS. The Asiatic Society was established by William Jones in 1784, and MRAS is an acronym for Member of the Royal Asiatic

[53] H.H. Wilson, *The Vishnu Puran: A System of Hindu Mythology and Tradition*, Trubner and Company, London, 1864.

Society. Specifically, in the meeting of the Royal Asiatic Society held on 13 November 1894, it was announced that Manmatha Nath Dutt had been elected a member.[54] Romesh Chunder Dutt became a member in 1893 and Manmatha Nath Dutt became a member in 1894. Romesh Chunder Dutt's address, as given in the membership details, was 30 Beadon Street and Manmatha Nath Dutt's was 65/2 Beadon Street. At the 28 March 1895 meeting of the Asiatic Society of Bengal, it was said, 'On an application from Babu Manmatha Natha Datta, a copy of his translation of the Ramayana was purchased, and the publications of *The Wealth of India* series, were subscribed for.'[55]

Name changes should not cause confusion. In 1784, the Society was established as Asiatick Society. In 1825, it became the Asiatic Society. In 1832, the name was further changed to The Asiatic Society of Bengal. Four years hence, it became The Royal Asiatic Society of Bengal, before it was finally changed to The Asiatic Society in 1951. Let us simply call it Asiatic Society. In 1849, Asiatic Society started publishing editions/translations under the Bibliotheca Indica Series. There were other books too, but translations were also part of the mandate. If one sticks to the kind of texts Manmatha Nath Dutt was interested in, there were numerous under the Bibliotheca Indica Series. For example, Asiatic Society published Sanskrit editions/translations of *Agni Purana* (1873–79, by Rajendralal Mitra), *Brihad Dharma Purana* (1888, by Haraprasad Shastri), *Brihad Naradiya Purana* (1891, by Hrishikesha Shastri), *Parasara Samhita* (1887, by Krishnakamal Bhattacharya), *Kamandakiya Nitisara* (1884, by Ramnarayana Vidyaratna and Rajendralal Mitra), *Kurma Purana* (1890, by Nilmani Mukhopadhyaya), *Markandeya Purana* (1904, by F.E. Pargiter), *Parasara Smriti* (1890, by Chandrakanta Tarkalankara),

---

54 Refer to <https://www.cambridge.org/core/journals/journal-of-the-royal-asiatic-society/article/i-general-meetings-of-the-royal-asiatic-society/3508D9B3D6D8D4F419823FA62AE7B113> (last accessed 2 January 2020).

55 *Proceedings of the Asiatic Society of Bengal, January to December 1896*, Asiatic Society of Bengal, 1897.

Sama Veda Samhita (1874–79, by Satyavrata Samasrami), *Varaha Purana* (1893, by Hrishikesha Shastri) and *Vayu Purana* (1880–81, by Rajendralal Mitra).[56] These works were all published in the same period, that is, the latter half of the nineteenth century.

Let us remember the name Nilmani Mukhopadhyaya. Most of these were edited Sanskrit texts, not English translations. But the Asiatic Society was interested in English language translations too and the works by Krishnakamal Bhattacharya and F.E. Pargiter were indeed translations. It would have been natural for the Dutt translations to be published under the Asiatic Society's Bibliotheca Indica Series. Why weren't they? Perhaps Manmatha Nath Dutt wasn't interested. Since he became a member of the Asiatic Society, this seems unlikely. It is much more likely that he wasn't taken seriously as a scholar, a point we will return to in Chapter 5. As the Rajendralal Mitra example illustrates, this couldn't have had much to do with formal training. Rajendralal Mitra (1823/24–1891), the first Indian president of the Asiatic Society, possessed no formal training in Sanskrit.

To get back to Manmatha Nath Dutt's society, this society published several authors, such as Horace Hayman Wilson on the Puranas, Sita Nath Datta (also known as Sitanath Tattvabhushan) on Adi Shankaracharya, translations of Kalidasa and Rammohun Roy on the Vedas.[57] After his death, Manmatha Nath Dutt suffered from

---

[56] For the complete list, refer to <http://www.sanskritebooks.org/2015/12/bibliotheca-indica-series/> (last accessed 2 January 2020).

[57] H.H. Wilson, *Puranas, or an Account of Their Contents and Nature*, Society for the Resuscitation of Indian Literature and Elysium Press, Calcutta, 1897; Sita Nath Datta, *Sankaracharya, His Life and Teachings: A Translation of Atma-Bodha*, Society for the Resuscitation of Indian Literature and Elysium Press, Calcutta, 1897; H.H. Wilson, *Dramas, or A Complete Account of the Dramatic Literature of the Hindus*, Society for the Resuscitation of Indian Literature and Elysium Press, Calcutta, 1900; *Works of Kalidasa – 1. Shakuntala [in the Translation of Sir W. Jones], 2. Vikrama-Urvashi [translated by H.H. Wilson], 3. Kumara-Sambhavam, 4. Megha-Duta [translated by H.H. Wilson], 5. Ritu-Samhara, 6. Raghu-Vamsha*, Society for the Resuscitation of Indian Literature and Elysium Press, Calcutta, 1901; and Roy, *Translations of Several Principal Books, Passages and Texts of the Veds, and Some Controversial Works on Brahmunical Theology*.

the lack of copyright legislation at the time. But, interestingly, he also benefited from the same when he was alive. For reprinting, there were no legal hassles.

Why give it the name Society for the Resuscitation of Indian Literature? This is speculation, but I think it may have been because of Dadabhai Naoroji's statement, 'The Benefits of British Rule'. Originally, this was written in 1871. However, Dadabhai Naoroji's collection of speeches, essays, addresses and writings was published in 1887, precisely when Manmatha Nath Dutt was going about naming his society.[58] One needn't mention Dadabhai Naoroji's complete documented balance sheet, the pluses and the minuses, the costs and benefits of British rule. Under the head in the cause of civilization, he said, 'Resuscitation of India's own noble literature, modified and refined by the enlightenment of the West.' This is probably where Manmatha Nath Dutt got the name of his Society. Dadabhai Naoroji's 1887 book also probably explains where Manmatha Nath Dutt got the name of his magazine. The essays had a section titled 'The Poverty of India'. However, so far as India's literature is concerned, India was hardly poor. Therefore, the magazine was called *The Wealth of India*. This was a monthly magazine solely devoted to the English translation of the best Sanskrit works, and was published between 1892 and 1908. Manmatha Nath Dutt was the editor and publisher and Girish Chandra Chackravarti was the printer. The Dutt translations were originally, before being brought out as books, serialized in *The Wealth of India*. Effectively, the monthly issues were bound and became books. But, it is not as if everything published by the Society and Elysium Press was first published in *The Wealth of India*. There were some books that were just published independently, as books.

To the best of my knowledge, no copies of *The Wealth of*

---

[58] Dadabhai Naoroji, *Essays, Speeches, Addresses and Writings*, Caxton Printing Works, Bombay, 1887.

India survive anywhere in India. A copy on microfilm existed with the New York Public Library. Through the good offices of the Indian Consulate in New York, I managed to procure a copy.[59] Unfortunately, it is damaged and it is not a complete set from 1892 to 1912. From 1892, we only have the first page, nothing more. This first issue is from July 1892 and announced *The Wealth of India* as 'A Monthly Magazine Solely Devoted to the Translation of Best Sanskrit Works.' It was edited and published by Manmatha Nath Dutt, who was described as the editor of the English Ramayana. The annual subscription for the magazine was ₹6. Since this was the first issue of the magazine, the Ramayana translation must have been published independent of the magazine. Indeed, among several books by Manmatha Nath Dutt, only translations were routed through *The Wealth of India*, and that too not every translation. From 1894, we have an undamaged set of the magazine, with breaks here and there, which takes us through *Vishnu Purana*, *Kamandakiya Nitisara*, *Markandeya Purana*, *Harivamsha*, *Mahanirvana Tantra* and *Agni Purana*.

Both magazine and society did not survive after Manmatha Nath Dutt. The initial books were printed by Girish Chandra Chackravarti, who was also the publisher, under the name of Deva Press, with an address of 65/2 Beadon Street. The subsequent ones were printed by H.C. Dass, but at times the publisher was also named Elysium Press; occasionally it was simply the society. However, the address of Elysium Press continued to be the same as that of Deva Press—65/2 Beadon Street. So, the question that arises is this: Was Deva Press bought over by Elysium Press? Was it renamed? Note that then, as is often the case now, the dividing line between printer and publisher is often a blurred one. The way I understand it is at that time, there was no legal requirement for a publisher to be registered in any way. However, for societies, there was the Societies Registration

[59] The copy of the microfilm is now kept at the Nehru Memorial Museum and Library (NMML), Delhi. Converted into a PDF, there is one copy with NMML and another one with the National Library, Kolkata.

Act of 1860 and for printing presses and books, there was the Press and Registration of Books Act of 1867. The Societies Registration Act of 1860 did not make the registration of societies mandatory. I don't think the Society for the Resuscitation of Indian Literature was ever registered. There was no legal need. Registration would have required seven members. At the Society for the Resuscitation of Indian Literature, there was just a single person. Manmatha Nath Dutt was the founder and everything else. It was however different for the Press and Registration of Books Act of 1867. According to this act, every printing press had to make a declaration to the government. Was Deva Press bought over by Elysium Press? Was it renamed? That doesn't follow. It continued to publish books independently and up until much later.[60] In the Calcutta of that day and age, printing/publishing had become a bit of a cottage industry and had exploded. Although declarations of returns from the mid-1890s show that Manmatha Nath Dutt was the owner of Elysium Press,[61] technically, it was still registered as a printing press, not as a publisher. However, every book did require the name of the publisher to be stated. Often, that was the Society for the Resuscitation of Indian Literature. At some point, Elysium Press moved to 40 Nayan Chand Dutt Street, and later to 3 Furriapukur Street. The society's address and Manmatha Nath Dutt's address also moved around, to those specific addresses. In that environment, Dutt was a bit of an entrepreneur too, establishing societies, magazines and publishing houses. However, Elysium Press did publish the odd book that was neither authored nor edited by Manmatha Nath Dutt.[62]

A society, a magazine and a publishing house, flourishing or

---

[60] A. Kaviratna (ed.), *The Charaka Samhita*, 4 Vols, Girish Chandra Chakravarti Deva Press, Calcutta, 1902–25 and Jagatmohini Chaudhuri, *Englande Sat Mash* (in Bengali), Deva Press, Calcutta, 1902.

[61] For example, the annual returns of printing presses in *Report on the Administration of Bengal*, 1898.

[62] S.L. Tandan, *Selected Men of Hindustan*, H.C. Dass, Elysium Press, 1902.

not, require financial resources. There were certainly monthly subscriptions to *The Wealth of India*. There were also donations to the society. However, since the appeal for donations to the society were rarely repeated in the books, one deduces these donations weren't essential. As a zamindar, had Manmatha Nath Dutt been from the Hatkhola family, like Bhupati, he would have had his own resources to dig into. He must certainly have been paid by Keshub Academy too. However, the primary resources probably came from elsewhere. Indeed, his soliciting of resources, and more on that in Chapter 5, suggests he wasn't from the Hatkhola lineage, or at least not from a wealthy branch of that lineage. This suggestion will be confirmed later, when we will see that he had nothing to do with the Hatkhola lineage and was actually born in what is now Bangladesh. He certainly wasn't a zamindar in the Calcutta 'Bhupati' mould.

The 1893 *Gleanings from the Indian Classics*, Vol. I, noted, 'This Little Book is Respectfully Dedicated as a Token of Gratitude by the Editor to His Highness Sir Veeracarala Vurma, Knight Commander of the Most Eminent Order of the Indian Empire, Maharaja of Cochin.' This was Kerala Varma-V, who ruled from 1888 to 1895. Kerala Varma-V visited Calcutta in 1893. The 1899 *Gleanings from the Indian Classics*, Vol. III was 'affectionately dedicated as a token of friendship to Babu Dharani Kant Lahiri Choudhuri, the most enlightened and seminar of Kalipur in the District of Maimansing'. Mymensingh is now in Bangladesh. The name is usually spelt as Dharanikant Lahiri Chaudhuri today. The Lahiri Chaudhuris were zamindars in Mymensingh, but they were divided into various sub-families. One of these was based in Kalipur. There is no need to ask if Dharanikant Lahiri Chaudhuri ever visited Calcutta. He travelled throughout the country and published a fairly thick travelogue in Bengali.[63] It stands to reason that he must have visited Calcutta. At that time, Calcutta

[63] Dharanikant Lahiri Chaudhuri, *Bharat Bhraman* (in Bengali), 1910. This seems to have been privately published.

was also the capital of British India. Therefore, there was more than one reason to visit Calcutta. The 1897 *Harivamsha* translation was dedicated to Sir Pratap Singh (1848–1925), Maharaja of Kashmir (spelt Cashmere in the dedication) 'as a token of appreciation of his Highness' sympathy for such works, his vast scholarship and liberality by his most obedient and humble servant and admirer'. There are also records to show that Pratap Singh had paid a visit to Calcutta in 1885–86. The 1901 book on the Buddha was dedicated to Sir Sayajirao Gaekwad III (1863–1939), the Maharaja of Baroda State 'as a token of highest esteem and admiration for his highness' many virtues, accomplishments and scholarly attainments'. Maharaja Sayajirao Gaekwad III visited Calcutta in 1883. The 1904 *Outlines of Hindu Metaphysics* was dedicated to Maharaja Krishnaraja Wadiyar IV (1884–1940), Maharaja of Mysore from 1894 to 1940 'as a token of sincere regards and high esteem for His Highness' culture and sympathy'. Krishnaraja Wadiyar IV visited Calcutta in 1894. My intention is not to categorically state that these were the only occasions when these Maharajas visited Calcutta. There must have been other occasions too. I simply wanted to stress that Manmatha Nath Dutt did not necessarily have to travel throughout the country to meet these maharajas. He had every opportunity of meeting them in Calcutta.

But I suspect he did visit Mysore. T.R.A. Thumboo Chetty (1837–1907) was, among other things, the first Indian chief judge of the Chief Court of Mysore. Manmatha Nath Dutt features in Thumboo Chetty's biography.[64] This particular section in the biography is titled, 'The Mysore Oriental Library and Mr M.N. Dutt'.

> As member in charge of the Education portfolio, Mr Thumboo Chetty interested himself in the work of the Mysore Oriental Library and publication of old Sanskrit books. In 1895, he made

[64] T. Royaloo Chetty, *A Brief Sketch of the Life of Raja Dharma Pravina T.R.A. Thumboo Chetty, C.I.E, Formerly Chief Judge and Officiating Dewan of Mysore*, Hoe & Co., Madras, 1909.

> the acquaintance of Mr Manmatha Nath Dutt, MA, MRAS, Rector of the Keshub Academy, whose translations of the great epics of India deserved encouragement. Mr Thumboo Chetty found in Mr Dutt an excellent friend, a great patriot and a scholar, reputed for Sanskrit learning, who remarked: 'A taste for for the great Sanskrit works of antiquity enshrining the wisdom and learning of the Hindus has been developing itself among the more advanced spirits of the West.' This is true [...]

For an acquaintance to become a friend, frequent interactions are needed, though these interactions would also be through correspondence. How did Thumboo Chetty and Manmatha Nath Dutt meet? Thumboo Chetty's biography does not mention any visits to Calcutta. While there is no reason why he shouldn't have visited Calcutta, but given the differences in ages and positions, it is much more likely that Manmatha Nath Dutt visited Mysore often. Incidentally, that remark attributed to Manmatha Nath Dutt is interesting, because those words are lifted from a prospectus we will encounter in Chapter 5.

THREE

ENGLISH AND SANSKRIT

The longest introduction by Manmatha Nath Dutt was in one of his earliest translations, that of the Valmiki Ramayana. After that, the introductions became short and terse, almost non-existent. In the introduction to the Valmiki Ramayana, the translation is described in the following words:

> The Ramayana in an English Garb [...] The immortal Epic of Valmiki is undoubtedly one of the gems of literature [...] indeed, some considering it as the Kohinur of the literary region, which has for centuries, and from a time reaching to the dim and far past been shedding unparalleled and undying halo upon the domain presided over by 'the vision and the faculty divine.' [...] Bharata, stoutly and persistently declining, despite the exhortations of the elders and the spiritual guides, to govern the kingdom during Rama's absence in the forest, and holding the royal umbrella over his brother's sandals, are personations of the *ne plus ultra* of fraternal love, and consummate and perfect ideals of their kind [...] Truly of the Ramayana it can be said in Baconian language that it has come home to the business and bosoms of all men [...] Ravana is remembered not only in consequence of the prominent part he plays in

the Ramayana, but also on account of his famous advice to Rama immediately before death—namely that the execution of evil projects should be deferred, but that good ones should be promptly executed—a very sage counsel doubtless, answering partially to Macbeth's observation on hearing of Macduff's escape: '[...] From this moment/The very firstlings of my heart shall be/The firstlings of my hand [...]' [...] Ah, who can say how many women have turned away in the budding prime of youth from the primrose path of dalliance, and have in preference followed virtue, who alone is truly fair [...] In it [the Ramayana], cosmogony and Theogony, the genealogies of kings and princes—of human and extra-human beings, of *Ashuras* and *Danavas*, of *Jakshas* and *Gandharvas*, and *Shiddhas* and *Charanas*; folklore and anecdotes and legends, and stories half-mythical and half-historical; descriptions of cities existing at a period long anterior to the age of Troy and Memphis, and the chronicles of kings that reigned before Priam and Busiris—all these with others too numerous to enumerate, have been woven into the mighty web and woof of the magic drapery evolved by the son potent art of Valmiki [...]Nay, we can perhaps safely go so far as to assert that very few amongst those Western scholars who have devoted their lives to the study of Sanskrit literature, have been able to enter into the spirit of that part of its vocabulary in which are couched those peculiarly Hindu ideas and sentiments that constitute the unique genius of the people. To translate, therefore, such a work as the Ramayana from the dead and indefinite Sanskrit into the living and real English, is, like unearthening a fossil and inspiring it with life; or rather like transferring a light from a bushel in which it has been hidden, to a mountain-top, so that men may behold it and the surrounding objects by help of its grateful rays. Surely, to render a work from a dead tongue into a living language and specially such a language as English with all its resources,

> is literally taking it from its narrow and circumscribed sphere of influence, and placing it before the world at large—in fact, making it the common property and heritage of all mankind.

The Introduction ends with an invocation:

> Let us, accordingly, begin by invoking Him whose presence can convert the foulest and the most unclean spot, pure and clean, 'like the icicle that hangs on Dian's temple,' or the hearts and aspirations of the Vestal Virgins, or pious saints ever engaged in meditating the Most High.

In this longish quote, there is quite a lot that is easy to miss. 'The vision and the faculty divine?' That's William Wordsworth in 'The Wanderer'.

> Oh! Many are the Poets that are sown
> By Nature; men endowed with highest gifts,
> The vision and the faculty divine.

Ne plus ultra? That could be from anywhere. After all, it does mean the ultimate example. But I think it was because Coleridge wrote a poem titled 'Ne Plus Ultra'. Business and bosoms of all men is from Francis Bacon's 'The Epistle Dedicatory'. 'I do now publish my Essays; which, of all my other works, have been most current; for that, as it seems, they come home to men's business and bosoms.' Macbeth is obvious. But Shakespeare features again, through Coriolanus.

> The moon of Rome, chaste as the icicle
> That's curdied by the frost from purest snow
> And hangs on Dian's temple.

Priam and Busiris in the same breath? This might be coincidence. Or, was this because of a familiarity with Edward Young's (1683–1765) plays? I can understand Priam or Busiris separately. But linked together, it suggests Edward Young.[65] It is a pity there weren't these

[65] I have in mind *Busiris, King of Egypt: The Revenge*, more than *Busiris, King of Egypt: A*

kinds of introductions in the subsequent translations.

Gleanings from the Indian Classics, Vol. I starts with:

What mortal now can harm
Or foemen vex us more
Through thee, beyond alarm
Immortal God, we soar.

This is from John Muir's (1810–1882) translations, published in 1879.[66] Among other stories, *Gleanings from the Indian Classics*, Vol. I tells us about Krishna, who has gone away to Mathura and there is an attempt to bring him back to Gokula. When they all came to his royal palace to take him back to his old haunts, he told them as Prince Harry told his boon companions: 'Presume not that I am the thing I was, I have turned away my former-self.' This sounds unnecessary and forced, but never mind. It is from Henry IV, Part 2.

Presume not that I am the thing I was,
For God doth know—so shall the world perceive—
That I have turned away my former self.
But, it is difficult to get away from Shakespeare.

In the same book, we also have the Shakuntala story, with a footnote. In fairness, Manmatha Nath Dutt was not the first, or the only one, to make this comparison. 'Here again the similarity of Shakuntala and Miranda is very much apparent. Miranda saw only her old father Prospero, so did Shakuntala her father Karna.'[67] *Gleanings from the Indian Classics*, Vol. II has the story of the Rani of Argal, with a description of the river Ganga.

Tragedy.

[66] John Muir, *Metrical Translations from Sanskrit Writers*, Trubner and Company, London, 1879. This quote is from 'Praise of Soma'.

[67] In an odd typo, Kanva is throughout Karna.

Mother of mighty rivers
Adored by saint and sage;
The much-loved peerless Ganga,
Famous from age to age.

The Rani and her maids were then surrounded by Muslim soldiers.

The fear was in her bosom
The Rani shed no tear;
And her eye resentful sparkled,
As the enemy drew near.
She stood there brave and scornful,
Her maids by her side;
And with undaunted calmness
The Ajodhya's chief defied.
The Rani shouted out:
Are there no Hindu clansmen,
No Hindu brother here,
To whom a Hindu mother
And a Hindu wife is dear?
If such there be, arouse ye
Stand forth, stand forth to aid,
By the gods I adjure you,
My curse on you is laid.

Abhai Chand and Nirbhai Chand help her and the Mahomedans fled.

But all rejoiced to see her,
And with one voice did tell
How the Rani and her maidens
Had fought so brave and well.

As for the Governor who had attacked the Rani of Argal, it was said:

When white with age
Still then be bore the shame,

That he had wielded weapon
Against a noble dame.

The influence of Thomas Babington Macaulay's 'Horatius' is hard to miss. In *Buddha, His Life, His Teachings, His Order*, Manmatha Nath Dutt gave his address as Elysium Bower, Baranagore. In those days, Elysium was a commonplace word among the English-educated classes. There used to be an Elysium Road; now it is known as Lord Sinha Road. But, Elysium Bower takes us straight to John Keats and 'Endymion'.

Finally, in *Domestic Duty*, he writes:

> True love must unite the heart and soul in such a way that they may appreciate properly the burden of the song:
>
> I set my life in your hand,
> Mar it or make it sweet,
> I set my life in your hand,
> I lay my heart at your feet.

This is not that common a song. Where did Manmatha Nath Dutt get this from? His source must have been the novelist Marie Corelli (née Mackay, 1855–1924). This song is quoted in her 1900 novel *The Master-Christian*, and Manmatha Nath Dutt must have picked it up from there. This gives us an idea about the wide-ranging reading interests of Manmatha Nath Dutt.

Table 3.1 states what we know from the books, not just the year of publication and the publisher, but also how Manmatha Nath Dutt described himself in each publication. A few different addresses of Manmatha Nath Dutt are mentioned here:

- 65/2 Beadon Street
- 40 Nayan Chand Dutt Street
- 3 Furriapukur Street
- Elysium Bower, Baranagore

THE

RAMAYANA.

TRANSLATED INTO ENGLISH PROSE FROM THE ORIGINAL SANSKRIT OF VALMIKI.

BĀLAKĀNDAM.

EDITED AND PUBLISHED BY

MANMATHA NATH DUTT, M. A.

Rector, Keshub Academy.

PRINTED BY

GIRISH CHANDRA CHACKRAVARTI,

DEVA PRESS, 65/2, BEADON STREET.

CALCUTTA.

1891.

WITH

HIS HIGHNESS' KIND PERMISSION

THIS WORK

IS MOST RESPECTFULLY DEDICATED

TO

H. H. FARZAND-I-KHAS-I-DOULAT INGLISHIA
MAHARAJA SAYAJI RAO GAEKWAR SENA KHAS
KHEL SHAMSER BAHADUR G. C. S. I.

AS A TOKEN OF

HIGHEST ESTEEM AND ADMIRATION

FOR

HIS HIGHNESS' MANY VIRTUES, ACCOMPLISHMENTS

AND

SCHOLARLY ATTAINMENTS

BY

THE AUTHOR.

GLEANINGS

FROM

INDIAN CLASSICS.

EDITED BY

MANMATHA NATH DUTT, M, A.,

Rector, Keshub Academy,

Editor of the English Translation of the Ramayana, Srimadbhagabatam and Vishnupuranam.

CALCUTTA:

AT THE DEVA PRESS.

1893.

Rs. 2/—

[JULY.]

VOL. I. PART I.

THE

WEALTH OF INDIA.

A MONTHLY MAGAZINE SOLELY DEVOTED TO THE ENGLISH TRANSLATION OF THE

BEST SANSKRIT WORKS

6256

EDITED AND PUBLISHED BY

MANMATHA NATH DUTT,

EDITOR OF THE ENGLISH RAMAYANA.

PRINTED BY

GIRISH CHANDRA CHACKRAVARTI,

DEVA PRESS, 65/2, BEADON STREET.

CALCUTTA.

1892.

SUBSCRIPTION IN ADVANCE,

RUPEES 6.

Table 3.1: Miscellaneous details mentioned in each of Dutt's books

Name of the book	Year of publication	Dutt's educational qualification or/and designation	Described as translator of/ author of
Ramayana	1891	MA, Rector (Keshub Academy)	
Gleanings from the Indian Classics, Vol. I	1893	MA, Rector (Keshub Academy)	Ramayana, *Bhagavata Purana*, *Vishnu Purana*
Ramayana, *Uttara Kanda*	1894	MA	
Bhagavad Gita	1895	MA, MRAS	
Bhagavata Purana	1896	MA	
Mahabharata	1895–1905	MA, MRAS, Rector (Keshub Academy)	Ramayana, *Bhagavata Purana*, *Vishnu Purana*, Bhagavad Gita
Vishnu Purana	1896	MA, MRAS, Rector (Keshub Academy)	Mahabharata, *Bhagavata Purana*, Bhagavad Gita
Kamandakiya Nitisara	1896	MA, MRAS, Rector (Keshub Academy)	Ramayana, Mahabharata, *Vishnu Purana*, Bhagavad Gita
Markandeya Purana	1896	MA, MRAS, Rector (Keshub Academy)	Ramayana, Mahabharata, Bhagavad Gita, *Bhagavata Purana*

Name of the book	Year of publication	Dutt's educational qualification or/and designation	Described as translator of/ author of
Gleanings from the Indian Classics, Vol. II	1897	MA, MRAS, Rector (Keshub Academy)	Ramayana, Mahabharata, *Bhagavata Purana*, *Vishnu Purana*
Harivamsha	1897	MA, MRAS, Rector (Keshub Academy)	Ramayana, Mahabharata, *Bhagavata Purana*, *Vishnu Purana*, *Markandeya Purana*, Bhagavad Gita
Ayurveda	1899	Preface was left unsigned	
Gleanings from the Indian Classics, Vol. III	1899	MA, Rector (Keshub Academy)	Ramayana, *Bhagavata Purana*, *Vishnu Purana*
Mahanirvana Tantra	1900	MA, MRAS, Rector (Keshub Academy)	Ramayana, Mahabharata, *Bhagavata Purana*, *Vishnu Purana*, *Harivamsha*, Bhagavad Gita
Posta	1900		
Buddha, His Life, His Teachings, His Order	1901	MA, MRAS, Shastri (without Dutt being mentioned)	
Agni Purana	1903	MA, MRAS, Shastri, 40 Noyan Chand Dutt's Street	Ramayana, Mahabharata, *Vishnu Purana*, *Bhagavata Purana*, Bhagavad Gita

Name of the book	Year of publication	Dutt's educational qualification or/and designation	Described as translator of/ author of
Outlines of Metaphysics	1904	MA, MRAS, Shastri, Elysium Bower, Baranagore	Ramayana, Mahabharata, *Buddha, His Life, His Teachings, His Order*
Domestic Duty	1905	MA, MRAS	Ramayana, Mahabharata, *Buddha, His Life, His Teachings, His Order, Outlines of Metaphysics*
Angiras Samhita	1906	MA, MRAS, Shastri, Rector (Keshub Academy)	Ramayana, Mahabharata, *Bhagavata Purana, Mahanirvana Tantra, Harivamsha, Agni Purana, Markandeya Purana*
Harita Samhita	1906	MA, MRAS, Shastri, Rector (Keshub Academy)	Ramayana, Mahabharata, *Bhagavata Purana, Mahanirvana Tantra, Harivamsha, Agni Purana, Markandeya Purana*
Ushanas Samhita	1906	MA, MRAS, Shastri, Rector (Keshub Academy)	Ramayana, Mahabharata, *Bhagavata Purana, Mahanirvana Tantra, Harivamsha, Agni Purana, Markandeya Purana*

Name of the book	**Year of publication**	**Dutt's educational qualification or/and designation**	**Described as translator of/ author of**
Yama Samhita	1906	MA, MRAS, Shastri, Rector (Keshub Academy)	Ramayana, Mahabharata, *Bhagavata Purana*, *Mahanirvana Tantra*, *Harivamsha*, *Agni Purana*, *Markandeya Purana*
Atri Samhita	1907	MA, MRAS, Shastri, Rector (Keshub Academy)	Ramayana, Mahabharata, *Bhagavata Purana*, *Mahanirvana Tantra*, *Harivamsha*, *Agni Purana*, *Markandeya Purana*
Samvarta Samhita	1907	MA, MRAS, Shastri, Rector (Keshub Academy)	Ramayana, Mahabharata, *Bhagavata Purana*, *Mahanirvana Tantra*, *Harivamsha*, *Agni Purana*, *Markandeya Purana*
Katyayana Samhita	1907	MA, MRAS, Shastri, Rector (Keshub Academy)	Ramayana, Mahabharata, *Bhagavata Purana*, *Mahanirvana Tantra*, *Harivamsha*, *Agni Purana*, *Markandeya Purana*

Name of the book	**Year of publication**	**Dutt's educational qualification or/and designation**	**Described as translator of/ author of**
Vrihaspati Samhita	1907	MA, MRAS, Shastri, Rector (Keshub Academy)	Ramayana, Mahabharata, *Bhagavata Purana*, *Mahanirvana Tantra*, *Harivamsha*, *Agni Purana*, *Markandeya Purana*
Daksha Samhita	1907	MA, MRAS, Shastri, Rector (Keshub Academy)	Ramayana, Mahabharata, *Bhagavata Purana*, *Mahanirvana Tantra*, *Harivamsha*, *Agni Purana*, *Markandeya Purana*
Shatapata Samhita	1907	MA, MRAS, Shastri, Rector (Keshub Academy)	Ramayana, Mahabharata, *Bhagavata Purana*, *Mahanirvana Tantra*, *Harivamsha*, *Agni Purana*, *Markandeya Purana*
Likhita Samhita	1907	MA, MRAS, Shastri, Rector (Keshub Academy)	Ramayana, Mahabharata, *Bhagavata Purana*, *Mahanirvana Tantra*, *Harivamsha*, *Agni Purana*, *Markandeya Purana*

Name of the book	Year of publication	Dutt's educational qualification or/and designation	Described as translator of/ author of
Vyasa Samhita	1907	MA, MRAS, Shastri, Rector (Keshub Academy)	Ramayana, Mahabharata, *Bhagavata Purana*, *Mahanirvana Tantra*, *Harivamsha*, *Agni Purana*, *Markandeya Purana*
Upanishads	1907	MA, Shastri, Rector (Keshub Academy)	Ramayana, Mahabharata, *Bhagavata Purana*, *Mahanirvana Tantra*, *Harivamsha*, *Agni Purana*, *Markandeya Purana*
Apastamba Samhita	1908	MA, Shastri, Rector (Keshub Academy)	Ramayana, Mahabharata, *Bhagavata Purana*, *Mahanirvana Tantra*, *Harivamsha*, *Agni Purana*, *Markandeya Purana*
Gautam Samhita	1908	MA, Shastri, Rector (Keshub Academy)	Ramayana, Mahabharata, *Bhagavata Purana*, *Mahanirvana Tantra*, *Harivamsha*, *Agni Purana*, *Markandeya Purana*

Name of the book	Year of publication	Dutt's educational qualification or/and designation	Described as translator of/ author of
Vishnu Samhita	1908	MA, Shastri, Rector (Keshub Academy)	Ramayana, Mahabharata, *Bhagavata Purana*, *Mahanirvana Tantra*, *Harivamsha*, *Agni Purana*, *Markandeya Purana*
Dharmashastras (in Sanskrit)	1908	MA, Shastri, Rector (Keshub Academy)	Ramayana, Mahabharata, *Bhagavata Purana*, *Mahanirvana Tantra*, *Harivamsha*, *Agni Purana*, *Markandeya Purana*
Dharmashastras, Vol. II (in English)	1908	MA, Shastri, Rector (Keshub Academy)	Ramayana, Mahabharata, *Bhagavata Purana*, *Mahanirvana Tantra*, *Harivamsha*, *Agni Purana*, *Markandeya Purana*
Garuda Purana	1908	MA, Shastri, Rector (Keshub Academy)	Ramayana, Mahabharata, *Bhagavata Purana*, *Mahanirvana Tantra*, *Harivamsha*, *Agni Purana*, *Markandeya Purana*

Name of the book	Year of publication	Dutt's educational qualification or/and designation	Described as translator of/ author of
Manu Samhita	1909	MA, Shastri, Rector (Keshub Academy)	Ramayana, Mahabharata, *Bhagavata Purana, Mahanirvana Tantra, Harivamsha, Agni Purana, Markandeya Purana*
Vedanta Sara	1909	MA, MRAS, Rector (Keshub Academy)	Ramayana, Mahabharata, *Bhagavata Purana, Mahanirvana Tantra, Harivamsha, Agni Purana, Markandeya Purana*
Rig Veda Samhita	1906–12	–	–

What did Manmatha Nath Dutt study? He possessed formal degrees. In his books, from 1891 to 1900, he described himself as MA, with MRAS added from 1895 onwards. It helps to first understand the education system that existed then. Three universities were set up in 1857, in Calcutta, Madras and Bombay. In 1882, a commission was set up to examine the Indian education system.[68] Even if one is not interested in Manmatha Nath Dutt, this makes for a fascinating read. It tells us what the system was like in 1882. The commission's report stated, 'The function of these Universities is that of examination, and not of instruction. The latter is conducted by

[68] Since this was headed by William Wilson Hunter, it is usually known as the Hunter Commission. See, *Report of the Indian Education Commission*, Superintendent of Government Printing, Calcutta, 1883.

the affiliated colleges and other institutions authorized to send up candidates for the university examinations.' This was a decentralized structure, modelled on systems prevalent in Britain. Before enrolling in any such college, the University of Calcutta conducted an entrance examination. The Education Commission tells us this entrance examination examined the prospective student in the following categories: (*i*) English; (*ii*) an optional language; (*iii*) Mathematics and (*iv*) History and Geography. After two years, there was a FA Examination. Since one is interested in Manmatha Nath Dutt, one is specifically interested in English and Sanskrit. To clear FA in English, the student had to study *King Lear, Julius Caesar* and *Merchant of Venice* by Shakespeare, some books from Milton's *Paradise Lost*, Keats' *Hyperion*, Burke's *Reflections on the French Revolution*, Morley's *Life of Burke*, Church's *Spenser* and Stopford Brooke's *Primer of English Literature*. For Sanskrit, it was *Kumarsambhavam*, *Meghadutam* and *Shakuntalam*. After another two years, a student appeared for the BA examination and after another one year, for the MA examination. The MA was the last examination. There was nothing beyond the MA degree at the time.[69] For the BA examination in English, the reading list had Shakespeare's *The Merchant of Venice*, *Macbeth*, *The Tempest*, *Hamlet* and *Henry V*, as well as selections from Wordsworth and parts of Spenser's *Faerie Queene*. For the MA examination, there was *Henry IV*, *Henry VIII*, *Coriolanus* and *Othello*. While the texts did vary a bit from year to year, this gives a general idea. The picture that has so far emerged is of an individual with an intimate knowledge of English literature, in particular, poetry. Before the Shastri *upadhi* in Sanskrit, Manmatha Nath Dutt obtained an MA degree. By implication, he obtained FA and BA degrees prior to that. For his FA, BA and MA, he must have opted for English as his

[69] To be accurate, there was a separate examination for something known as the Premchand Roychand Studentship, instituted at the University of Calcutta in 1866. To sit for this examination, one needed to first obtain an MA degree from the University of Calcutta. An individual who obtained this studentship wrote PRS after his/her name.

subject of choice, though this can never be proved conclusively, using only this argument. After all, one can study Bengali or Philosophy, and still pick up one's knowledge of English. But English seems extremely likely. At the moment, in our style of probing, this is only a hypothesis. However, it is a hypothesis we will soon confirm and prove conclusively.

From the time of passing the entrance examination, it took five years to complete these degrees, at least in the University of Calcutta. 'The usual age at which an Indian student seeks admission to the University is between sixteen and eighteen years.'[70] Under normal circumstances, a student received the MA degree between the ages of 21 and 23. We know that from 1891, Manmatha Nath Dutt started to use MA after his name. If he started his translations immediately after passing the MA examination, say in 1888, he would have been born between 1865 and 1867. However, it must have taken a couple of years or more to get the magazine and the society going. Something like 1865 seems a more reasonable year of birth. To add to this, in 1888, he was already headmaster of Keshub Academy, as is evident from the compilation *A Poetical Reader*, though this book did not mention the MA degree. But to become a headmaster, he must have obtained the degree. Thus, 1866 or 1867 are probably ruled out—1865 is possible.

This means he would have taken admission at the university sometime around 1880, after passing the entrance examination. Where might he have studied? Let us think of his close contemporaries, friends and acquaintances who wrote those essays on Raja Rammohun Roy in 1896. Sitanath Tattvabhushan studied in General Assembly's Institution, which became Duff College in 1863 and Scottish Church College in 1908. Brajendra Nath Seal also studied there. Mohini Mohun Chatterjee also studied at the University of Calcutta, but I haven't been able to pin down the college. Nor have I been able

[70] The Hunter Commission.

to pin down the college for Nagendra Nath. Ghosh. Bipin Chandra Pal studied in Presidency College. Swami Vivekananda (Narendranath Datta, 1863–1902), a contemporary of Manmatha Nath Dutt, studied in General Assembly's Institution, though he initially spent a year in Presidency College. For Manmatha Nath Dutt, the options were thus Hindu College (which became Presidency College in 1855), General Assembly's Institution (which became Scottish Church College in 1908) and Metropolitan Institution (which became Vidyasagar College in 1917). Had it been even a decade later, Manmatha Nath Dutt, or someone of his background, would probably have studied in Metropolitan Institution. In 1880, that was possible, but not very likely.[71] That more or less pins it down to Presidency College or Scottish Church College. He must have taken his FA, BA and MA examinations from either of these two institutions. In 1880, Scottish Church College was still Duff College and students had to read the King James's Bible in college. Though this is a very tenuous argument, Manmatha Nath Dutt's familiarity with the Bible is suggestive more of Scottish Church College than of Presidency College. Scottish Church College would have made him more or less a classmate of Swami Vivekananda, just a couple of years younger. There is, however, a fallacy in the argument about Scottish Church College. There is no rule that states that the FA and the MA would have to be through the same educational institution. To eliminate the suspense, we will see that it was part General Assembly's Institution and part Metropolitan Institution, or to use their present-day names, part Vidyasagar College and part Scottish Church College.

Let us also mention a common link between those close contemporaries, friends and acquaintances who wrote essays on Raja Rammohun Roy in 1896—Sitanath Tattvabhushan, Brajendra Nath Seal, Mohini Mohun Chatterjee, Bipin Chandra Pal, Nagendra Nath

[71] One should not mix up that part of Metropolitan Institution that was a school with that part of Metropolitan Institution that was a college. For instance, Swami Vivekananda (Narendranath Datta) went to the school, but not the college.

Ghosh and Manmatha Nath Dutt. Since they wrote those essays on Raja Rammohun Roy, it is fairly obvious that they must have had some links with the Brahmo Samaj, as many educated Bengalis did then. Indeed, Sitanath Tattvabhushan was a member of the Brahmo Samaj. So was Brajendra Nath Seal.

> When Brajendranath studied at the General Assembly Institution, his teachers were amazed at this mathematical aptitude. In 1878, he was admitted into the college department of the same institution. Here among his classmates and friends was Narendra Nath Dutt, the future Vivekananda. Both of them evidently attended Sadharan Brahmo meetings, but whereas Brajendranath stayed with that community as an initiated member, Naren Dutt went on to Keshub's New Dispensation and later beyond that to found his own movement.[72]

Moreover,

> Of all the proponents of the theological position among the Sadharans after the schism of 1878, none was more effective a spokesman and prolific a writer than Sitanath Tattvabhusan. Born in a Sylhet village in 1856, Sitanath later endured persecution and loss of ancestral property when he chose to become a Brahmo. Arriving in Calcutta for the first time in 1871, he immediately joined the other young students who sat at the feet of Keshub Sen in the Brahmo Niketan.[73]

Bipin Chandra Pal was born in a village called Poil in Habiganj district, which now falls under the Sylhet division in present-day Bangladesh. Bipin Chandra Pal's autobiography *Memories of My Life and Times*[74] didn't cover the final years of his life, but it did cover the initial years.

---

[72] David Kopf, *The Brahmo Samaj and the Shaping of the Modern Indian Mind*, Princeton University Press, Princeton, NJ, 1979.

[73] Kopf, *The Brahmo Samaj and the Shaping of the Modern Indian Mind*.

[74] Bipin Chandra Pal, *Memories of My Life and Times*, Yugayatri Prakashak, Calcutta, 1932.

He writes of the time when he was still studying in Sylhet:

> A few days later, when, I think, I was reading in the fourth class of the Sylhet Government School, Sita Nath Datta, who has since made his mark as a religious thinker and writer and is well-known among the members and sympathisers of the Brahmo Samaj and others interested in liberal religious thought as Pandit Sita Nath Tattvabhusan, came and joined our class. He belongs to our own district. But as his uncle was living in Calcutta and had a shop of hardware things in Burrabazar, Sita Nath had his early education in the Metropolis. One of his cousins, Babu Sree Nath Datta,[75] an old and well-known member of the Church of the New Dispensation had already come under the influence of Keshub Chunder Sen and had publicly joined the Brahmo Samaj. Young Sita Nath was already something of a Brahmo when he came and took his admission in our class in the Sylhet Government School.

The autobiography has a chapter titled, 'How I Came to the Brahmo Samaj'. This leaves Nagendra Nath Ghosh, Mohini Mohun Chatterjee and Manmatha Nath Dutt. There is a reference to Nagendra Nath Ghosh in Bipin Chandra Pal's autobiography.

> The 'Bengal Public Opinion' was under a new name really the old 'Brahmo Public Opinion' started as the official organ of the Sadharana Brahmo Samaj [...] It was very largely patronized by the advanced sections of educated Bengalees, and men like the late Mr. Nagendra Nath Ghoshe, Barrister-at-Law and Principal of the Metropolitan Institution, were regular contributors to the columns of this paper.

---

[75]A Bengal directory was published in 1879 and this describes Srinath Datta as a deputy inspector of schools in Maunbhoom (Manbhum), now the district of Purulia. This must have been the same Srinath Datta. See, *The Bengal Directory 1879*, Thacker, Spink and Company, Calcutta, 1879.

While this does not directly say that Nagendra Nath Ghosh was a member of the Brahmo Samaj, it is certainly implied. Mohini Mohun Chatterjee was also a remarkable person.

> Mohini, originally a member of the Brahmo Samaj, became Madam Blavatsky's (1831–1891) secretary, but eventually separated from the Theosophical movement. In 1885 Mohini introduced the *Gita* to the future Nobel Prize winning Irish poet William Butler Yeats (1865–1939). Yeats, a Dublin Theosophist, also had a positive encounter with Rabindranath Tagore in 1910, wrote a poem about his friend Mohini, and associated with Gerald Heard before the latter became a member of the Vedanta Society in Southern California.[76]

If all these friends and acquaintances were members of the Brahmo Samaj, at least initially, it is reasonable to presume that so was Manmatha Nath Dutt.

But we have moved away from Manmatha Nath Dutt's education. The proposition was that he studied in Scottish Church College or Presidency College, probably the former. What about the school? Before probing that, we need to ask a different question. Where was he born? Was he born in, or around, Calcutta? Was he born into the Hatkhola Dutta family? Or, was he born elsewhere, in what is now Bangladesh, and did he move to Calcutta later, to study in college? The question of a school in Calcutta arises in the former case, not in the latter. Let us think of the schools in Calcutta. Though the feeder school to Sanskrit College is possible, given his proficiency and expertise in English, the answer probably boils down to Hare School (established in 1818), or Hindu School (established in 1817), or Oriental Seminary (established 1829). Hare and Hindu were government schools, while Oriental Seminary was private. Perhaps, one should also remember the following. First, among

---

[76] Gopal Stavig, *Western Admirers of Ramakrishna and his Disciples*, Advaita Ashrama, 2010.

the Bengali *bhadralok*, because of Henry Louis Vivian Derozio and the Young Bengal movement a few decades earlier, Hindu School had become less favoured. Second, Oriental Seminary was famous for the quality of its education in English. For example, the noted Shakespearean scholar, Captain D.L. Richardson taught there. Third, though Rabindranath Tagore dropped out of any system of formal education, he did study for a while in Oriental Seminary and that's not completely irrelevant. The student strength in a school now is completely different from what it was then. The Hunter Commission tells us that in 1881–82, the average number of pupils in a school in Bengal was 17. Had Manmatha Nath Dutt studied in Oriental Seminary, Rabindranath Tagore would certainly have known him personally, as a co-pupil. Fourth, there was a reference to Soshee Dutt earlier. Romesh Chunder Dutt was a bit older than Manmatha Dutt and we know nothing about the interaction between the two kin families, if that is what they were. Is it possible that Soshee Chunder Dutt also planted the love for English poetry in Manmatha Nath Dutt? In any event, forced to identify the school, one would perforce opt for either Oriental Seminary or Hare School. At that time, Hare School was favoured by the families of a lot of educated Bengalis, though Oriential Seminary is also possible. However, there is an even more likely possibility, of his not having been born in Calcutta at all and of not having studied in a Calcutta school. The exploration about a school in Calcutta is unnecessary.

In seeming contradiction of what I suggested earlier, there is a strong possibility that Manmatha Nath Dutt wasn't born in Calcutta at all. Nor was he from the Hatkhola lineage. There are several reasons for this hypothesis. First, in accounts of those who were from the Hatkhola lineage, such as Romesh Chunder Dutt or Hirendranath Dutta (more on whom later), Manmatha Nath Dutt never finds a mention in them. All references to him are by marriage. His ancestors did not seem to exist in the Calcutta of that time. Second, anyone from the Hatkhola lineage would have been reasonably comfortable financially, if not downright wealthy. While this does fit the portrayed character of Bhupati, it doesn't fit the image of Manmatha Nath Dutt going around, searching for funders for his books. Manmatha Nath Dutt (W) wasn't Manmatha Nath Dutt (Z). Indeed, in Chapter 5, we will talk about his attempts to tap the government for funds. Third, many prominent members from the Hatkhola lineage went to university to study and subsequently obtained law degrees, or joined the civil services. Let us consider two examples, both Manmatha Nath Dutt's contemporaries. Hirendranath Dutta (b. 1860), who completed his BA and MA in English from Presidency College, did law and joined the Calcutta High Court. Romesh Chunder Dutt (b. 1848) too studied in Presidency College, before going abroad to study, and then joined the civil services. Manmatha Nath Dutt tried to do none of these. His profession, so to speak, was limited to becoming Rector of Keshub Academy. This may have been a matter of personal choice, but it also possible that such options were foreclosed because of his background. That is, he wasn't all that comfortable financially and was not from the Hatkhola lineage. Fourth, consider this bit on the description of the Hindu wife taken from *Gleanings from the Indian Classics*, Vol. II.

> The soft rays of the morning sun play on the wavy breast of the beautiful river that flows towards the sea through the fertile plains of Ind [*sic*]. The green leaves of innumerable trees on both the banks stoop down towards the water, as if to give her a parting kiss. Narrow winding paths from the neighbouring houses come through the silvan vistas to the very edge of the water. Along these paths the Hindu wife goes back home with her pitcher of water. The villagers move away from her path and respectfully stand by to let her pass [...] Graceful female forms are often seen passing along the village paths and the village afternoons are always sweetened with the music of their ornaments [...] She is the mother of all the children of the

> neighbourhood and her love flows like an autumnal river that overflows its banks and inundates the country.

This is a description of village India, rural Bengal to be precise. Is anyone who has been born and brought up in Calcutta likely to write this? This may seem a very tenuous argument, as indeed it is. Surely, a person who has been born in Calcutta and has been brought up there can travel to rural Bengal. That is perfectly true. But, which parts of Bengal? The western parts, what is West Bengal today, or the eastern parts, now part of Bangladesh? The village and the river could have been from anywhere in rural Bengal. But a river which flows towards the sea through the fertile plains of the country? Think of the rivers in West Bengal now, and there are some major ones. For these, no writer is likely to use the expression 'flows towards the sea'. However, Bangladesh is full of such rivers. Indeed, in Bangladesh, rivers flowing towards the sea is almost a default option. Despite being a tenuous argument, Manmatha Nath Dutt might very well have been born in the eastern parts of Bengal, moving to Calcutta to study in college.

As mentioned earlier, Sitanath Tattvabhushan/Dutta and Bipin Chandra Pal had known each other from Sylhet. Nagendra Nath Ghosh was born in Chittagong. There were several from what is now Bangladesh who studied in Calcutta and got drawn towards the Brahmo Samaj. Among the prominent ones, there were Monomohun Ghose, Durga Mohun Das, Dwarkanath Ganguli and Jagadish Chandra Bose from Bikrampur, Prafulla Chandra Ray from Jessore, Ananda Mohun Bose from Mymensingh, Prosanna Kumar Roy from Dacca and Nagendranath Chatterji from Barisal.[77] However, it wasn't an easy transition to Calcutta, especially if one was drawn towards the Brahmo movement with parents who were not Brahmos.

---

[77]Kopf, *The Brahmo Samaj and the Shaping of the Modern Indian Mind.*

> It was the boys from rural East Bengal who seem to have suffered the most in their struggle to emancipate themselves most from the diehard conservatism of parents, relatives, and neighbours [...] Their arrival in the city compelled Keshub Chandra Sen to establish the Brahmo Niketan in 1871 as a sanctuary for boys who in most cases had been cut off from family, caste, and village society [...] Here Sitanath Tattvabhusan, for one, future theologian and philosopher, was first given a home after leaving behind him his family in Sylhet [...] The persecution of Brahmos seems to have been extreme in East Bengal.[78]

There was more.

> As a student there, he experienced a new type of persecution. He was jeered at by West Bengal boys for being a rustic 'Bangal' from the East [...] an experience reminiscent of others in Calcutta experienced by Bipin Chandra Pal, Prafulla Chandra Ray, and Nirad Chaudhuri—all from East Bengal.[79]

Bipin Chandra Pal wrote:

> I do not know how things are now; but in my young days, students in Calcutta colleges, who came from East Bengal Districts, and particularly in the Presidency College, which was patronized by the sons of the aristocracy in Calcutta, had a rather bad time of it, [e]specially if they were very sensitive. Their local patois was the object of open ridicule by their more refined metropolitan fellow-students.[80]

---

[78]Kopf, *The Brahmo Samaj and the Shaping of the Modern Indian Mind.*

[79]Kopf, *The Brahmo Samaj and the Shaping of the Modern Indian Mind.* This particular quote is about Krishna Kumar Mitra studying in Presidency College. However, it comes across in several autobiographies.

[80]Pal, *Memories of My Life and Times.*

Faced with discrimination, such students preferred to stay in their own messes. For instance, when he first arrived as a student in Calcutta, Bipin Chandra Pal stayed in a mess that predominantly housed students from Sylhet. These messes eventually led to associations being formed. That is how Bipin Chandra Pal and Sundari Mohan Das (1857–1950) set up the Srihatta Sammilani (Sylhet Union) in Calcutta in 1876. Bipin Chandra Pal and Sundari Mohan Das had been classmates in Sylhet. In his autobiography, Bipin Chandra Pal also writes: 'Sundari Mohan Das had been a class-mate of mine ever since the establishment of the Government School in Sylhet in 1868 or '69; but there was hardly any special intimacy between us.'[81] That intimacy developed later.

Habiganj, once known as Habibganj after its 'founder', Syed Habib Ullah, is now a district in Bangladesh. It is in the north-east corner of Bangladesh. There is a broader Sylhet region, right next to Meghalaya, Assam and Tripura. Due to trade, commerce and tea plantations, Sylhet has always been prosperous. Indeed, the word Sylhet is itself a corruption of the word Shrihatta, meaning prosperous settlement, or prosperous trading centre. In today's administrative structure within Bangladesh, there is a Sylhet division and that is further subdivided into Habiganj, Moulvibazar, Sunamganj and Sylhet districts.

When one uses the word Sylhet, there are multiple layers of meaning. With shifting geographical and administrative boundaries, in the past there was a broader historical region known as Sylhet, but today, there is the Sylhet division and Sylhet district—the latter a part of Sylhet division. Sylhet has had a chequered history, with different turning points in its separate constituent parts. But whatever be the geographical definition of the area known as Sylhet, by 1835, the entire area was under the control of the East India Company.

---

[81] Pal, *Memories of My Life and Times.*

There is a long-forgotten book by the odd title of *Sylhet Thackeray*.[82] This was a biography of William Makepeace Thackeray, not the famous novelist, but his grandfather. The grandfather, who had the same name as the grandson, was the first Resident of Sylhet and therefore, came to be known as 'Sylhet Thackeray'. Historically, after 1765 (when part of Sylhet came under British administration) and 1835 (when all of Sylhet came under British administration), Sylhet was sometimes pulled in the direction of Assam and sometimes in the direction of Bengal. As part of the British administration, it was first part of the Bengal Presidency. With the stated intention of facilitating development and more revenue collection in a backward area like Assam, as a relatively prosperous region, Sylhet was made part of the Chief Commissioner's Province of Assam in 1874. When Bengal was divided in 1905, Sylhet became part of Eastern Bengal and Assam. However, in 1912, it was delinked from Bengal again and made part of the Chief Commissioner's Province of Assam. These subsequent periods of history do not concern us. The district (zila) of Habiganj has several upazilas (sub-districts) now. The village of Poil, which is where Bipin Chandra Pal was born, is in Habiganj Sadar upazila whereas Sita Nath Datta was born in the village of Sangar in Baniachong upazila. Baniachong and Habiganj are next to each other.

The school that Bipin Chandra Pal mentioned—Sylhet Government School—was one of the oldest schools of the region. What's relevant for our purposes is that a lot of students from Sylhet used to go to Calcutta to study in the second half of the nineteenth century. A system of English education was introduced in the schools of Sylhet. There were steamer services and railways. The Assam Bengal Railway connected Sylhet (and Assam) with the port in Chittagong, though that was somewhat later, in the last decade of the nineteenth century. But, why was Sylhet integrated

---

[82] F.B. Bradley-Birt, *'Sylhet' Thackeray*, Smith, Elder and Company, London, 1911.

with Assam in 1874? As mentioned previously, this was because Assam was backward and Sylhet was relatively prosperous, and integrating a relatively more prosperous region would have ensured revenue for Assam. School education had been also introduced in Sylhet. But when Bipin Chandra Pal studied, there was no college in Sylhet. Murari Chand College was the first college in Sylhet which was established in 1892. Students wishing to study beyond school had to go elsewhere. And because Sylhet was relatively backward, there was a system in place whereby the government provided scholarships to students to study in Calcutta.

> In 1874 Sylhet was separated from Bengal, upon the institution of the province of Assam under a Chief Commissioner. Assam was regarded as a very backward province, and the Government thought it necessary to offer special encouragement to the people by allotting a large number of scholarships to students passing the University Entrance Examination from the Assam schools. This is how, though I passed the Entrance Examination without any manner of distinction at all, I secured a monthly scholarship of rupees ten and came and took my admission in the Presidency College at Calcutta as a 'scholar' or scholarship-holder.[83]

If Bipin Chandra Pal got a scholarship to study in Calcutta, there is no reason why Manmatha Nath Dutt should not have, just a few years later. This argument stretches the point too much. However, the argument is not so much about a scholarship. When students go elsewhere to study, they often follow a herd mentality, even today. For instance, when several students from present-day Kolkata go to a specific educational institution in Delhi to study, other students follow. This is because the presence of networks makes new students more comfortable and a pattern begins to develop. I gave the

---

[83] Pal, *Memories of My Life and Times.*

example of Sylhet, but I am making a broader point about the eastern parts of Bengal. Transport connectivity was improving and this included transport connectivity to Calcutta. Schools were being set up in the eastern parts of Bengal and students began to enrol in these schools, to learn English. However, colleges were set up a couple of decades later. Therefore, students from the eastern parts of Bengal often came to Calcutta to study, after taking the entrance examinations. Other than Sylhet, Mymensingh and Barisal also didn't have colleges at the time. Chittagong was the only exception. The first college in Mymensingh, known then by the name of City College, was set up in 1878. Barisal's first college, Brojomohun College, was established in 1889. Chittagong College was established in 1869. The argument is not about Manmatha Nath Dutt having been specifically from Sylhet, but from somewhere that is now in Bangladesh. That might explain why we have no clear statements about his parentage. We don't know for sure that he became a Brahmo, though he was certainly close to those who were Brahmos. The possibility of consequent distancing from parents was greater for a son born in what is now Bangladesh than for a son who was born in Calcutta. If Bipin Chandra Pal's experience is any indication, orthodox parents reacted very strongly to sons becoming Brahmos and marrying Brahmo women. Fathers and mothers cut off their sons, denied them the right to perform funeral rites and disinherited them from property. Manmatha Nath Dutt was probably a Brahmo, though we haven't quite proved it yet. He certainly married a Brahmo lady. The proposition of parents, in what is now Bangladesh, cutting him off is very plausible.

There is a piece of information that can now be thrown in, and this completely clears up the mystery about our translator's education and birth. A certain 'Manmathanath Datta', aged 16, cleared the undergraduate entrance examination of the University of Calcutta in

1881 and was placed in the second division.[84] We know this from Calcutta university's calendars. This particular Manmathanath Datta would therefore have been born in 1865. This person cleared his entrance examination from Pabna Zila School. In 1883, he passed the FA examination through the General Assembly's Institution and was placed in the second division. Through Metropolitan Institution, this Manmathanath Datta cleared his MA examination in English in 1888, again securing second division. I wish to reiterate that the number of individuals who opted for higher education then was low. There could not have been several Manmatha Nath Dutts at the same time. We got to know about Manmatha Nath Dutt (D). Now we know about Manmatha Nath Dutt (W). No other individual with the name Manmatha Nath Dutt figures in the University of Calcutta records. Manmatha Nath Dutt (Z) probably did not go to university. Thus, Manmatha Nath Dutt (W) was from Pabna, now in Bangladesh.

The *Pabna District Gazeteer*, published in 1923, has a fair bit of information about Pabna.[85] At that time, before the railways were built, there was a road from the headquarters of Pabna town to Kushtia in Nadia district. The distance was 127 miles. Therefore, Calcutta wasn't that far.

> The first institution for the teaching of English started by Government in the district was the Pabna Zila School. It was established in 1853 as a Government English school. The Hindus, quick to perceive the great advantage which [the] knowledge of English literature and science would give them, eagerly availed themselves of the opportunity of acquiring a knowledge of western subjects taught in the Government

[84] Calcutta university calendar, 1882–83. Thacker, Spink and Company published these calendars, on behalf of the university.

[85] L.S.S. O'Malley, *Bengal District Gazetteers, Pabna*, Bengal Secretariat Book Depot, Calcutta, 1923.

> institution, and also started schools of their own on similar lines, receiving aid from Government for their maintenance.[86]

This was the school Manmatha Nath Dutt went to. But the first college in Pabna was set up in 1898. Therefore, after passing out of school, Dutt would have had to go elsewhere for an education.

To tie up the loose ends, let us recapitulate what we already know. First, Manmatha Nath Dutt was born in 1865. Second, he had nothing to do with Hatkhola. He wasn't born in Calcutta. He was born in what is now Bangladesh. Third, he studied in Pabna Zila School, which is a very old school. The *Pabna District Gazeteer* is partly right about this school. It was originally set up in 1836 and became a government-funded public school in 1853. This is the school where Jagadish Chandra Bose (1858–1937), a few years Manmatha Nath Dutt's senior, also studied. Fourth, Pabna district is full of rivers—Padma, Icchamati, Baral and Jamuna. When he wrote about rivers flowing towards the sea, Manmatha Nath Dutt might very well have been describing the Padma, or the Icchamati. Fifth, he studied English. Sixth, he did his FA through General Assembly's Institution and his MA through Metropolitan Institution. In 1888, he was ready to start with his ventures. Note that this in itself was somewhat unusual. Within two years of having obtained an MA degree, the average Bengali *bhadralok* did not start an entrepreneurial venture—a printing press and a publishing house. He could not have had a family background in printing presses or publishing either, as the first proper newspapers and printing presses in Pabna were started a few decades later. However, he could have had a family background in business and entrepreneurship.

Let us not forget the Bengali novel either. That was published in 1885, when Manmatha Nath Dutt was 20. We can now understand the reason for the use of the expression 'boy author'. Novels,

---

[86] O'Malley, *Bengal District Gazetteers*.

especially first novels, can often be autobiographical. Since I haven't been able to get a copy of the novel, the gist of the plot will have to be gleaned from the review mentioned earlier. *Bangali Meye* [Bengali girl] is the story of a young girl (Sarala) who is in love with a young man (Indra Nath). Sarala's father (Hara Kumar Mitra) is not averse to the match. But since Indra Nath's father isn't interested, Hara Kumar Mitra gets his daughter married off to someone else. In a spirit of self-sacrifice, succumbing to her father's wishes, Sarala (the *Bangali meye* in question) accepts. We are told that Indra Nath collected subscriptions 'on the occasion of Babu Surendra Nath Banerji's imprisonment' and that Indra Nath had passed 'the Entrance and First Arts Examinations'. Surendranath Banerjee (1848–1925) was imprisoned in 1883. Manmatha Nath Dutt passed the Entrance examination in 1881 and the FA examination in 1883. It is indeed autobiographical.

Though I haven't been able to get a copy of the original novel, *Bangali Meye*, I did manage to get a revised reprint, known as *Bangali Bou*.[87] This was published in 1892 and clearly stated that it was a revised edition of *Bangali Meye*, with a couple of additional chapters. We can now fill in a few more of the autobiographical details, if that is what they are. Hara Kumar Mitra resides in a village in Pabna, on the other side of the Padma. He frequents meetings of the Brahmo Samaj, though he is not quite a member. He is a minor zamindar, prone to oppressing his tenants. Indra Nath Sinha is a kayastha and he is his father's only son. His mother died while he was still a child. As a student, Indra Nath Sinha lives along with a few friends in a rented house in Simla, outside Calcutta.[88] The autobiographical elements fit to a T, including the resemblance between the names Manmatha Nath and Indra Nath, not to mention the obvious kayastha and Pabna connections. There is nothing special

[87] *Bangali Bou* (in Bengali), New Calcutta Press, Calcutta, 1892.

[88] Simla is in Hooghly district.

about the novel and one can understand why the reviewer trashed it. There are two bits that are odd though. First, *Bangali Meye* clearly had the name Manmatha Nath Dutt as author. *Bangali Bou* was published anonymously. Why was it published anonymously? True, *Bangali Meye* had received a bad review, but that's not a convincing enough reason. Was it because Manmatha Nath Dutt wasn't married when the first edition was published in 1885, but was married when the second edition was published in 1892? Second, should one attach any special significance to the year 1892? Did it have something to do with Charubala's death? As we shall see later, his wife, Charubala, probably died in 1891.

One can also make some educated guesses about his family background. Bengali kayasthas in Pabna worked for the government, or were zamindars, talukdars or jotdars. Modern industry came to Pabna later and Bengali kayasthas did not typically work for the indigo or jute industries. A detailed description of Pabna was published in Bengali in 1923.[89] This is in six volumes and has a wealth of information, including names of prominent families, such as zamindars. For a son to study in Calcutta, Manmatha Nath Dutt's father must have been one of those zamindars and must have been mentioned in these six volumes. As a prelude, one should know that there was a famous peasant uprising in Pabna between 1873 and 1876, with the peasants (ryots) complaining against oppression by the zamindars. These landlords were often those who obtained tracts courtesy the Natore Raj. Sujanagar is part of Pabna district. In the fifth volume of the Radharaman Saha series, we find the only reference to a family named Datta, in all of Pabna. There were Dattas in other parts of eastern Bengal, but in Pabna, these were the only prominent ones. They lived in a largish village known as Sagarkandi, within Sujanagar.

[89] Radharaman Saha, *Pabna Jelar Itihas* (The History of Pabna District), Pustak Bipani, Calcutta, 1923.

In brief, let us recapitulate what the series states. A cluster of villages is known as Sagarkandi. It is about 27 miles from the district headquarters of Pabna. The Datta kayastha family of Sagarkandi is famous and influential. The ancestors, Govindacharan Datta and Gurucharan Datta, were probably brothers. They made a fortune as contractors during the laying of the lines of the Eastern Bengal Railway. (The first line from Calcutta to Kushtia was laid in 1862, and this was extended up to Goalundo Ghat in 1865.) With this money, they bought a lot of property and came to be known as zamindars. During the rebellion by the peasants, there was a lot of oppression by this Datta line of zamindars, somewhat reminiscent of Hara Kumar Mitra's behaviour. Thereafter, Govindacharan Datta's descendants sold off the property in Sagarkandi, bought property in Calcutta, and moved there. (This would have been around 1876.) Gurucharan Datta's descendants remained in Sagarkandi. At the time when this was written, in 1923, Gurucharan Datta and his younger brother, Janakinath Datta, were both dead. The descendants of Gurucharan Datta and Janakinath Datta were known as the zamindars of Sagarkandi. One of Janakinath Datta's sons, Dvijendranath Datta, was a lawyer and practised in Calcutta High Court. Bengali sons often have names that are similar to those of their fathers, especially in the second part of the name. The timelines are just about right for Manmatha Nath Dutt to have been Janakinath Datta's son.

In 1876, William Hunter authored a detailed description of Pabna.[90]

> The existence of Pabna, as a separate District, dates only from 1832 [...] Lying at the point of the angle formed by the convergence of the Ganges and the Brahmaputra, it commands

---

[90] William Hunter, *A Statistical Account of Bengal*, Vol. IX (on Murshidabad and Pabna), Trubner and Company, London, 1876. Most of this volume was about Murshidabad. It also mentions that in 1876, there were only eight members of the Brahmo Samaj in Pabna, 'of whom all but one are natives of other Districts'.

> the two river highways of Eastern India. Its marts, often of mushroom growth, have become centres for collecting and re-distributing the exports and imports of rich provinces; and the Sirajgunj merchants transact, on an arid riverbank, half the jute trade of Bengal.

To explain what I said about Natore Raj earlier,

> According to local tradition, the members of the family of the Raja of Nattor were once the sole proprietors of all the *pargana*s comprised in Pabna District at the time of its formation in 1832 [...] During the incumbency of the latter [Raja Ram Krishna], almost all the family estates fell into arrears, and were bought, at the public sales, partly by the Raja's agents and servants, and partly by the ministerial officers of Government, the Tagores of Calcutta, and others, who are the present proprietors of the estates.

The Dutt family belonged to the 'others' category and was not important enough to find a mention in William Hunter's description of the Pabna agrarian disturbances of 1873. He writes:

> These are the two original causes of the dispute—a high rate of collection as compared with other *pargana*s, and an uncertainty as to how far the amount claimed was due. The third auxiliary cause is to be found in the violent and lawless character of some of the *zamindar*s, and of the agents of others.

The five main families of zamindars involved in these disputes were the Tagores of Calcutta, the Bandopadhyayas of Dacca, the Sandyals of Salap, the Pakrashis of Shal and the Bhaduris of Porjana. Among these, it was only the Tagores who handled the dispute well and fairly.[91] However, the Radharaman Saha volume does mention

[91] Though not specific to Pabna, Romesh Chunder Dutt's 1874 book, sympathetic to the cause of riots highlighted the issues. See, Romesh Chunder Dutt, *The Peasantry of Bengal*,

oppression by the Dutt zamindars of Sagarkandi.

We have veered away from the educational qualifications that pertain to Sanskrit. From 1901, 'Shastri' was added to Manmatha Nath Dutt's name. The fact that the title 'Shastri' was added later means that it was a separate degree. Where did he study and how did he acquire this title? Let us get Pali out of the way first. It is necessary to mention this because there are occasional suggestions that he translated from Pali too. He did not translate from Pali. But he may have known Pali. He suggests in the Preface to *Buddha, His Life, His Teachings, His Order*. 'In presenting this sketch of the life and teachings of this Great Teacher I have consulted almost all the works extant either in Sanskrit or Pali.' However, we will talk about the Buddha book later. Consulting works in Pali may have been a bit of an exaggeration. The Buddha book was primarily based on secondary sources. Regarding the Shastri title, it might certainly have been an honorary degree, explaining Sucheta Kriplani's statement, 'In those days the Indian States often organized conferences of scholars and honoured them with titles and other rewards.'[92]

What if it was not honorary and what if 'Shastri' simply meant that he studied Sanskrit? The gurukula and traditional systems are somewhat different in nature. In the modern system, the upadhi, or the title 'shastri', connotes different things at different places. Today, the nomenclature will be Shastri for a BA in Sanskrit, Acharya for an MA, Vidyavaridhi for a PhD and Vachaspati for a DLitt. We tend to forget that Lal Bahadur Shastri's (1904–1966) surname was not Shastri. Shastri was the upadhi. Lal Bahadur Shastri's surname was Srivastava, which he dropped because of its caste connotations. Subsequently, when he did a BA (not in Sanskrit) from Kashi Vidyapith in 1925, he obtained the title of 'Shastri'. Today, there

---

Thacker, Spink and Company, London, 1874.

[92] Kripalani, *An Unfinished Autobiography.*

are Sanskrit universities where BA confers on the successful student the title of 'Shastri'. Sanskrit College was established in Calcutta in 1824,[93] with an affiliated school that was like a feeder school. In the initial years, Sanskrit College had a secretary, not a principal. In both 1832 and 1833, the officiating secretary was Horace Hayman Wilson (1786–1860). Horace Hayman Wilson left a deep impression on Manmatha Nath Dutt and the latter drew extensively on Wilson's work, not just for his translation of the *Vishnu Purana*. Ishwar Chandra Vidyasagar (1820–1891) was the principal from 1851 to 1858. Before Vidyasagar, only brahmana students could join Sanskrit College. Manmatha Nath Dutt was not a brahmana. He was what in Bengal is called a kayastha. During Vidyasagar's tenure as principal, the admission rules were changed and non-brahmana students were allowed to enrol in Sanskrit College. Subsequently, Mahesh Chandra Nyayratna Bhattacharyya (1836–1906), who was the principal from 1876 to 1895, introduced the system of upadhi. Note that the University of Calcutta did not have a Sanskrit department until 1907. Therefore, when Manmatha Nath Dutt became Shastri in 1901, the MA degree would have been awarded by the University of Calcutta, but the title of 'Shastri' would have been conferred by Sanskrit College. Naturally, this is under the assumption that 'Shastri' was a studied degree.

Having obtained the title, one had the option of dropping the original surname, as Sivanath Sastri (also spelt Shibnath Shastri) did. However, other than the Buddha book, Manmatha Nath Dutt never dropped his original surname. Coming back to Sivanath Sastri (1847–1919), he was author, historian, educationist, social reformer and much more. He was Manmatha Nath Dutt's senior by almost 20 years and there is no reason why they should have interacted, though Manmatha Nath Dutt would have known of, even if not personally, Sivanath Sastri. Born Sivanath Bhattacharya, Sivanath Sastri

[93] In 2016, Sanskrit College became a university.

dropped the surname after obtaining the title 'Shastri'. A footnote in his autobiography[94] tells us how he obtained the title. Sivanath Bhattacharya passed the MA in Sanskrit examination through the University of Calcutta with a first class. This is also confirmed in Sivanath Shastri's biography, authored by his daughter, Hemalata Devi.[95] That is how he obtained the upadhi of Shastri. He studied in Sanskrit Collegiate School and Sanskrit College.

That's exactly what happened with Haraprasad Shastri (1853–1931), born as Haraprasad Bhattacharya. He studied in Sanskrit College and Presidency College and stood first in the first class in the MA examination in Sanskrit, leading him to obtain the title of 'Shastri'. Subsequently, he dropped the surname of Bhattacharya. Thus, if 'Shastri' was a studied degree, that should establish Manmatha Nath Dutt studied in Sanskrit College for his MA in Sanskrit, was first class first and thus obtained the upadhi of 'Shastri', assuming that he studied his Sanskrit in Calcutta. This was a remarkable accomplishment, though he would have studied for the MA in Sanskrit when he was a bit older than most other students. Note that Sanskrit College and Presidency College had close links and were just across the road from each other on College Street. But, had 'Shastri' been a studied degree, Manmatha Nath Dutt might have been taken more seriously as a scholar by, say, the Asiatic Society or by the experts called in by the Home Department (more on that later). Therefore, it is extremely likely that Shastri was an honorary degree, in line with Sucheta Kriplani's statement, and not a studied degree. One of the various maharajas conferred that title on him.

---

94 *Atmacharit* was published in Bengali by the Sadharan Brahmo Samaj in 1918.

95 Hemalata Devi, *Pandit Shibnath Shastris Jiban-charit* (in Bengali), New Era Publishing, Calcutta, 1919.

FOUR

A BIT ON ROADS

There is a Manmatha Dutta Road in Calcutta. It is in the area known as Belgachia and connects Jessore Road with Tara Sankar Sarani. Towards the Tara Sankar Sarani end, a fork leads to Indra Biswas Road. Manmatha Dutta Road is a short road and there is nothing along the road—neither a statue not a plaque—to indicate who it was named after. The road has been there for years, and even featured in many Bengali short stories. The famous poet Kazi Nazrul Islam (1899–1976) lived in Manmatha Dutta Road for some years and old-timers still point out his residence as a landmark. Typically, roads are named after famous or important people, and there certainly aren't too many famous people named Manmatha Dutta. Towards the end of the nineteenth century and the beginning of the twentieth, there were famous Bengalis with the same first name of Manmatha Nath. For instance, Manmatha Nath Ray Chowdhury and Manmatha Nath Gupta, and there was more than one Manmatha Nath Ghosh. But Manmatha Nath Dutta was a rarity.

Mohun Bagan Athletic Club, the football team, had a glorious decade in the 1930s and towards the start of that decade a Dr Manmatha Dutta played for Mohun Bagan and captained it. But there is no logical reason why a road in Belgachia should be named after him. There was also a freedom fighter named Manmatha Datta. In the Andaman Cellular Jail, there are plaques with names of freedom fighters, neatly arranged by way of decade and region. For the 1932–38 period in the Bengal list, a Manmatha Datta is numbered 190. That road in Belgachia is unlikely to be named after him either. Therefore, it is almost a certainty that this road is named after Manmatha Nath Dutt (D), Manmatha Nath Dutt (W) or Manmatha Nath Dutt (Z). It was too early (1937) for either the freedom fighter or the footballer to have a road named after them.

Kolkata Municipal Corporation has a Road Renaming Committee, as do many other cities in the country. From a book by Thankappan Nair, we know how this road came to be named.[96] Let us consider Indra Biswas Road first, which was named after a local zamindar as a mark of respect.

> The proposal to name the road from the 'projection of the Triangular Road extending from the end of Manmatha Dutt Road, running parallel westwards also at the back of the Pareshnath Temple as Indra Biswas Road' was notified by the Corporation on August 25, 1937 (C.M. Gaz.; September 4, 1937, p. 631) and the name was sanctioned on April 28, 1938 (C.M. Gaz., May 7, 1938, p. 878).

Moving on to Manmatha Dutt Road:

> The Corporation, vide notification dated August 25, 1937, proposed that a 'portion of the new road to the east of the Tallah Park running from 16-2, Paikpara Raja Manindra Road to the junction of the three roads southwards to the north of the Pareshnath Temple' be called Manmatha Dutt Road (C.M.

---

[96] P. Thankappan Nair, *A History of Calcutta's Streets*, Firma KLM, Calcutta, 1987.

Gaz., September 4, 1937). The name was sanctioned on April 28, vide notification issued in the C.M. Gaz, of May 7, 1938, p.878.

We need to understand how this part of Calcutta came to be developed. These were the northern suburbs of the city. Today, Kolkata Municipal Corporation (KMC) has almost 150 wards. These are the geographically contiguous wards, say number 1 to 6. This locality consisting of the Chitpur and Cossipore areas was outside KMC's purview till 1923, though from 1889, Chitpur and Cossipore were under a suburban municipality. Today, Cossipore is Ward No.1, Belgachia is Ward No.3 and Chitpur is Ward No.6. Manmatha Nath Dutt Road is in Ward No.5. The proposal to name the road Manmatha Dutt Road was dated 25 August 1937. Since Manmatha Nath Dutt died in 1912, as has been deduced, 1937 would have been his 25th death anniversary. This was a convenient date to commemorate him, if that was the intention. It could well have been that. At that time, the mayor of the KMC was Sanat K. Roy Chowdhury, and a mayor might have had a role to play in naming of roads. Sanat K. Roy Chowdhury also had an important role to play in the Bengal Provincial Hindu Mahasabha. In addition, he was the author of a monograph on Hinduism.[97] He was interested in Chandi. The worship of Chandi is based on the *Markandeya Purana*, a text Manmatha Nath Dutt translated. Sanat K. Roy Chowdhury would probably have been interested in Manmatha Nath Dutt (W). Did Manmatha Nath Dutt really die in 1912? In all probability, the answer is yes. He might of course have decided to give everything up and go off on *sanyasa*. However, the abrupt way in which the *Rig Veda* translation was terminated does suggest that he died in 1912, somewhat unexpectedly. It was a sudden death. No succession planning had been done.

---

[97] Sanat K. Roy Chowdhury, *Hinduism and Eternal Verities*, Bhupendra Chandra Lahiri, Calcutta, 1928.

But there is no means of categorically stating that Manmatha Nath Dutt Road is named after Manmatha Nath Dutt (W). It could also be Manmatha Nath Dutt (D) or Manmatha Nath Dutt (Z). I am inclinded to think it is a toss-up between Manmatha Nath Dutt (W) and Manmatha Nath Dutt (D), probably the latter. In the Nona Chandanpukur area of Barrackpore, there is a school named Manmatha Nath High School. In the same area of Nona Chandanpukur, there is also a hospital named Biraj Mohini Matri Sadan. I suspect these are named after Manmatha Nath Dutt (D) and Biraj Mohini Mitra/Dutt, respectively.

There is a Bengali website abasar.net[98]—*abasar* meaning leisure. This website seems to have antecedents in a monthly magazine, also known as *Abasara*. An old listing of Bengali magazines tells us the editor of *Abasara* from 1314 to 1317 was Nabakumara Dutt, from 1317 to 1321 was Surenchandi Dutt, from 1321 to 1322, the post was jointly held by Lalbihari Dutt and Sharacchandra Ghosh, and finally from 1322 to 1323, Sharachhandra Ghosh was its editor. It is important to note that these are years as per the Bengali calendar—1314 is 1908 and 1323 is 1917. Writing for the Absara website on 30 August 2016, Dilip Das gave us an account of what the old *Absara* was like. The first issue was printed in 1904 and the last issue was printed around 1917. Like Manmatha Nath Dutt, we know nothing about the first editor, Nabakumar Dutt. He died in 1912 and his son, Surenchandi Dutt, took over. However, Surenchandi Dutt also died early, when he was only 23 years old. Therefore, in 1915, Surenchandi Dutt's paternal uncle (his father's younger brother), Lalbihari Dutt, replaced him.[99] And he was succeeded by someone from outside the family

[98] Refer to <http://www.abasar.net/> (last accessed 2 January 2020).

[99] The Hatkhola Duttas were into printing and publishing, though usually in Bengali, not English. For example, Prananath Dutta (1840–1888) and his younger cousin, Girindrakumar Dutta (1841–1909) were from the Hatkhola Dutta family and published an illustrated Bengali monthly magazine known as *Basantaka*. Girindrakumar Dutta was a minor novelist who wrote in Bengali.

called Sharacchandra Ghosh. In other words, Nabakumar Dutt was Manmatha Nath Dutt's brother's son and both paternal uncle and nephew died in the same year, 1912. That's a bit of a coincidence. Dilip Das makes a comment about this old magazine. Not only was it neutral, it was also indifferent to the events that went on at the time. It completely ignored them, especially stuff that was political. This was also true of Manmatha Nath Dutt (W) and his writings. The uncle/father may have written in English, while the nephew/son wrote in Bengali. But they shared this common trait. Jnanendra Kumar's collations also tell us that a zamindar named Lalbihari Dutt spent a lot on public works, though Manmatha Nath Dutt's name doesn't figure in that context. Let us pause for a moment to reflect on what Jnanendra Kumar and the Absara website have collectively told us: (*i*) Manmatha Nath Dutt was descended from the Hatkhola Dutt family; (*ii*) Manmatha Nath Dutt's son was Lalbihari Dutt; (*iii*) Manmatha Nath Dutt was married to Shibnarayan Basu's daughter; (*iv*) Lalbihari Dutt spent a lot on public works; (*v*) Lalbihari Dutt edited a monthly Bengali magazine and (*vi*) since Shibnarayan Basu did not have any sons, he left all his property to Lalbihari Dutt, his daughter's son. So, the question that remains is—which Manmatha Nath Dutt is this? Is this Manmatha Nath Dutt (W)? Or, is this a description of Manmatha Nath Dutt (Z)?

There is a conundrum. Is this Manmatha Nath Dutt from the Hatkhola Dutt family or our Manmatha Nath Dutt? Though we have mentioned Pabna, let's put that on hold for a moment. Since the Hatkhola Dutts were everywhere and since Manmatha Nath Dutt is not that common a name, it is tempting to deduce this is our Manmatha Nath Dutt. Indeed, it is tempting to deduce that every Dutt was, in one way or another, related to the Hatkhola Dutt family. But consider this, in that day and age, even if it was a second marriage, was it likely that our Manmatha Nath Dutt would have married someone (Shibnarayan Basu's daughter) who was older than him? This is no doubt possible, but does seem implausible. In those days, Manmatha Nath Dutt wasn't an unknown name. Writing just a few years later, wouldn't Jnanendra Kumar have mentioned Manmatha Nath Dutt's contributions, instead of just referring to him in passing as Lalbihari Dutt's father and Shibnarayan Basu's son-in-law? Think of those who we know were Manmatha Nath Dutt's friends, acquaintances and contemporaries—Sitanath Tattvabhushan, Brajendra Nath Seal, Mohini Mohun Chatterjee, Bipin Chandra Pal and Nagendra Nath Ghosh. Not only were they Brahmos, or close to those who were Brahmos, their default language of expression was English. It is not that they did not write in Bengali, nor is it the case that they did not know Bengali. But their preferred language was English. If Jnanendra Kumar's Manmatha Nath Dutt is our Manmatha Nath Dutt, we have his son (Lalbihari Dutt) editing a monthly Bengali magazine and writing for it. This doesn't quite fit. The conundrum is best resolved by delinking our Manmatha Nath Dutt from the Hatkhola lineage entirely. Many of his friends and acquaintances were from the eastern parts of Bengal. And so probably was he. He had nothing to do with Hatkhola. Our Manmatha Nath Dutt came to Calcutta to study and stayed on. In his initial years, as happened with a lot of Bengalis exposed to Western education, he was attracted towards the Brahmo Samaj movement. But, as we argued earlier, he was from Pabna. The descriptions from Jnanendra Kumar and the *Absara* website are about Manmatha Nath Dutt (Z), and have nothing to do with Manmatha Nath Dutt (D) or Manmatha Nath Dutt (W).

In the initial years, Manmatha Nath Dutt gave his address as Beadon Street or Nayan Chand Dutt Street. But later, such as in the 1904 metaphysics book, his address was changed to Baranagore. Manmatha Nath Dutt provided four different addresses in his publications: (*i*) 65/2 Beadon Street; (*ii*) 40 Nayan Chand Dutt Street; (*iii*) 3 Furriapukur Street and (*iv*) Elysium Bower, Baranagore. Elysium Bower was clearly the name of a house and Baranagore is too broad an area to pin down in any way. A minor point about Keshub Academy though. Normally, though not invariably, Manmatha Nath Dutt described himself as the rector of Keshub Academy.[100] The Keshub Academy in question is off Beadon Street (Ward No. 26). The address is actually 147/G, Ramdulal Sarkar Street. But this was later. In some earlier descriptions from the late 1890s, Keshub Academy is described as having been located at 65 Beadon Street. This was Manmatha Nath Dutt's residential address. The school probably started in what was his home, before it moved elsewhere. Today, Keshub Academy is a government school and it isn't surprising that it maintains no records of its past. There are no records of past rectors. So, Beadon Street is the area where Manmatha Nath Dutt lived, and worked, for a large part of his life, until 1909, when Manmatha Nath Dutt described himself as rector, Keshub Academy.

Sitanatha Tattvabhushan (1856–1945), born Sitanath Dutta, was an extremely influential writer. Initially close to Keshub Chandra Sen, he eventually joined the Sadharan Brahmo Samaj and became its official theologian and secretary, before becoming president of the Sadharan Brahmo Samaj. In 1900–01, he delivered a series of lectures on Vedanta before the Theological Society, Calcutta. In 1909, these lectures were published in the form of a book,[101] in which Sitanath Tattvabhushan was described as headmaster, Keshub Academy. A rector is a bit like a principal. However, it is certainly possible for a school to have both a rector and a headmaster. But that seems unlikely, especially if someone of the stature of Sitanath Tattvabhushan is involved. It is much more likely that in 1909, Manmatha Nath Dutt ceased to be rector of Keshub Academy and the nomenclature rector was replaced by the term 'head master'. Also, it is possible that he moved to Baranagore because he no

---

[100] For example, the *Agni Purana* translation and the Buddha book are exceptions to this rule.

[101] Sitanath Tattvabhushan, *The Vedanta and Its Relation to Modern Thought*, H.C. Das, Elysium Press, Calcutta, 1909.

longer needed to be close to the school. Baranagore/Baranagar is part of Kolkata now. It used to be the outskirts then. At that time, Baranagore would have reminded people of Ramakrishna Math and Swami Vivekananda.

I have previously mentioned the *Bengal Directory 1879.*[102] What does it say about these addresses? The directory had a street directory with the names of its prominent residents. Brojomohun Dutt and Madhublall Dutt were residents of 2 Beadon Street, Brindabun Dutt was a resident of 50 Beadon Street, Opendronath Dutt was a resident of 74 Beadon Street, Gunganarain Dutt 'and natives' lived in 83 Beadon Street and Tarineychurn Dutt was a resident of 87 Beadon Street. Those were the various Dutts who lived in Beadon Street. The year was 1879, roughly 10 years before Manmatha Nath Dutt came to reside in that locality. From 63 to 65 Beadon Street, there were 'huts, stables and shops', though 66 Beadon Street had Beadon Press, Doyalchand Baparee and shop. Urban transformation can be rapid. In 10–15 years, that hut/stable would have become a proper house, school and printing press. As for Nayan Chand Dutt Street, it is mentioned as Nyan Chand Dutt Lane and Sumbhoochurn Banerjee lived at 40 Nyan Chand Dutt Lane. Moteelall Dass was a resident of 3 Farriapooker Street. Had Manmatha Nath Dutt been a member of the Hatkhola lineage, would he have lived in a house that was described as consisting of 'huts, stables and shops', albeit a few years earlier? As mentioned, many Dutts lived in proper houses along Beadon Street, some of whom were undoubtedly from the Hathkola family. A Dutt from that lineage need not have lived in a hut or stable. So, what was this Beadon Press, located in 65 Beadon Street? According to the records, there was also Elm Press, located in 63 Beadon Street. Beadon Press does not seem to have published any books after 1885. Was it bought over by Manmatha Nath Dutt? Did it become Elysium Press, located in 65/2 Beadon Street?

---

[102] Tattvabhushan, *The Vedanta and Its Relation to Modern Thought.*

I explored the addresses—65/2 Beadon Street, 40 Nayan Chand Dutt Street and 3 Furriapukur Street. Fariapukur (Furriapukur) is an area near Belgachia in north Calcutta. Furriapukur Street has become Shibdas (Sibdas) Bhaduri Street. Shibdas Bhaduri was the famous football player who was Mohun Bagan's captain when Mohun Bagan defeated East Yorkshire Regiment in 1911 and won the IFA Shield. This is Mohun Bagan territory, with Mohun Bagan Row, a souvenir shop named 'Striker' and several sports shops. But, 3 Shibdas Bhaduri Street (3 Furriapukur Street) is a disappointment. It is a gift and toy shop, certainly twenty-first century Kolkata and not nineteenth century Calcutta.

Beadon Street is however a different matter. This stretch of Beadon Street is now Abhedananda Road. Further down, it becomes Dani Ghosh Sarani. Oriental Seminary isn't far away, nor is Keshub Academy. Suddenly, you are in the midst of old Calcutta. The roads become narrower, vehicles rarer. Every third house is an old one—dilapidated, abandoned, unoccupied. They loom on like eerie ghosts from some bygone past, single-storied, double-storied, sometimes even three-stories high. But, where is 65/2 Beadon Street? I can't find it. The numbers aren't sequential.

Along comes a postman, astride his bicycle. There can't be a better person to ask! He points me in the right direction. Yes, there is a 65/2 Beadon Street. Someone lives there too. No, he has no idea who lives there. No, he has never delivered letters to anyone there. Following his directions, I identify a very small grocery store. Ah, yes! 65/2 Beadon Street. 65/2B Beadon Street is the house next to the grocery store. Someone does live there. I think to myself bang on the door and someone will emerge. I look up at the two-storied house, made of wood. The upper floor is falling apart. There is a large metal yellow demolition notice from the KMC on the front door, proclaiming 'Dangerous/risky house'. Grass and weeds are sprouting from the threshold and the lintel. The adjacent house, also falling apart, shows no signs of occupancy either. That must have been

65/2A Beadon Street and the two together would have been 65/2 Beadon Street. A very large house, perhaps six rooms on the first floor and six on the ground floor. Perhaps a printing press and an office did exist on the ground floor, with living rooms on the first floor. Dare I bang on the door of 65/2B Beadon Street? What if the house falls down? I bang, and a lady emerges, 30-something in age. I explain what I want. What do I want? I want to know who owns the house, what are its antecedents? By now, a small group of around six curious onlookers has gathered, with two street dogs for company. 'I don't know', the lady says. 'Let me call my mother-in-law.' The mother-in-law emerges, 60-something in age. 'We have been here for the last 50 years', she says. 'We don't own the house. No one does. There was a gentleman named Chandrasekhar Gupta. He used to run hospitals. But they ran into losses and the government took them over. When Chandrasekhar Gupta died, he had no heirs. He never married. My family used to work for Chandrasekhar Gupta and we have stayed on. I have no idea if Chandrasekhar Gupta owned the house. We will stay here until the Municipal Corporation kicks us out.' I have a strong urge to explore the house, venture upstairs. But the state of the house and the state of the stairs deter me.

It is now time to explore 40 Nayan Chand Dutt Street. Nayan Chand Dutt Street is quite unlike what it appears on Google Maps or Google Earth. It is a very narrow U-shaped road. It emerges from Beadon Street, meanders and again emerges on Beadon Street, right next to what would have been 65/2 Beadon Street. I go back and forth, but there is no 40 Nayan Chand Dutt Street that I can locate. It ends at 38 Nayan Chand Dutt Street. Like Manmatha Nath Dutt himself, 40 Nayan Chand Dutt Street does not seem to exist, except in the books. However, it might have existed. At the corner, where 65/2 Beadon Street would have ended, had there been another house, it would have been 40 Nayan Chand Dutt Street. Perhaps 40 Nayan Chand Dutt Street eventually became part of 65/2 Beadon Street and the two houses were combined. As I walk up and down Nayan Chand Dutt Street, I find a man sunning himself and ask him about 40 Nayan Chand Dutt Street. 'There is no such house', he remarks. 'I have been here for a long time. Nayan Chand Dutt Street ends at number 38. Do you want to buy an old house?' Since I have no such intention, he loses interest. 'Ask the tea-stall owner. He has been here for 30 years. He has seen the times when mutton used to be one paise a kilo.' The tea-stall owner is very uninterested, but volunteers the information that there is a really old man who lives in a house further down. He might know. I go and knock at the door of that house. 'My father is sleeping', he responds. 'He is almost 90. It is time for his afternoon nap.' When I request him to ask his father, I am summoned in. This is also an extremely old house, falling apart. I climb upstairs gingerly. The staircase is damp and dark. There is a very old grandfather clock ticking away. 'I was born in 1930', the gentleman says. 'When I was young, I heard my father mention Manmatha Nath Dutt as a famous author. No, we never had his books at home. Most of the houses in this neighbourhood have no valid property papers. No one knows who owns them. Ours is one of the few houses that has valid papers. We bought it legally. But we have no money to repair the house and the municipal corporation has served us with a demolition notice. Since the houses don't have property papers, they can't be bought or sold. Like me, these houses will also die, some day.'

Most of Beadon Street is dead now. The vibrancy of Kolkata is elsewhere. It is hard to imagine that in the second half of the nineteenth century, the vibrancy of Calcutta was here, in and around Beadon Street. This was Calcutta's Drury Lane, in more senses than one. Kolkata's Star Theatre is now in Bidhan Sarani (Cornwallis Street). The old Star Theatre, demolished by the Calcutta Improvement Trust in 1931, was in 68 Beadon Street. From 65/2 Beadon Street, the site is less than a stone's throw away. Great National Theatre was in 6 Beadon Street, later replaced by Minerva Theatre in 6/1 Beadon Street. Bengal Theatre used to be where the Beadon Street Post Office is now. Emerald Theatre, which lasted from 1887 to 1896, was in 68 Beadon Street. Though Rimli Bhattacharya's book on Binodini Dasi is about the actress and her autobiography, there is good documentation of the theatres that developed around the Beadon Street area at the time.[103]

[103]Binodini Dasi, *My Story and My Life as an Actress* (edited and translated by Rimli Bhattacharya), Kali for Women, Delhi, 1998.

FIVE

THE HOME DEPARTMENT REBUFF

The National Archives of India have some files from the second half of the nineteenth century. The antecedents of the National Archives are to be found in the Imperial Records Department, established in Calcutta in 1891. There are Home Department files and Manmatha Nath Dutt figures in some of the correspondences preserved in these files. 'A' category files were those that were always preserved since they were important. 'B' category files were secondary in importance. Some were preserved, others discarded. Manmatha Nath Dutt merited 'B'. Therefore, several files are missing, or have been destroyed, and I have been able to get access to only a few. As happens with government files, there is a chronological stringing together of this file too, beginning from April 1890 and ending with September 1898. Therefore, though some files are missing, one can broadly reconstruct the sequence of events. The subject matter of the initial set of files is 'patronage to Babu Manmatha Nath Dutt's English translation of Sanskrit works'. The last set of files is specifically 'patronage to his edition of *Kamandakiya Nitisara*'. These files amplify and modify the tentative hypotheses advanced in the earlier chapters. Since this is a completely different and new data source, it belongs in a different chapter.

These files are invaluable because, for the first time, we have access to a 'Prospectus' for Oriental Publications that was issued by Manmatha Nath Dutt, MA, MRAS, Rector of Keshub Academy. A long quote is in order.

> A taste for the great Sanskrit works of antiquity enshrining the wisdom and learning of the Hindus, has been developing itself among the more advanced spirits of the West since the time when Sir W. Jones surprised European scholars by his translation of Kalidasa's *Sakuntala.*[104] The seeds thus sown falling into good ground has yielded an abundant harvest, and Western *savants* following in the wake of Sir William, have enriched their respective literatures by appropriating to their demesnes thoughts and sentiments bequeathed by the ancient Hindu authors. America has also taken up the tale, and her sons now yield to none in their appreciation of the high worth of oriental studies and in the enthusiasm they display for them. On the other hand, the Hindus of the present day are growing daily more and more alive to the importance of Sanskrit literature. Progress, to be intrinsic, must obey the universal Law of Evolution—and in order that the modern Hindus of today may make real advance to the destined goal of Humanity towards which all nations are marching from different sides, they must proceed on the lines laid down by their forefathers, and vitalize the old things into new forms in harmony with the times. So great is the significance of our ancient literature—and fortunate it is that the educated portion of the community is rousing itself from the apathy in which, after the positive antipathy of the preceding era, it had lain for years; and is regarding Sanskrit learning with an eye of love and reverence. Now that

[104] Part of this sentence was mentioned by Thumboo Chetty. In 1789, William Jones translated it as *Sacontalá or The Fatal Ring: An Indian Drama by Cálidás* Translated from the Original Sanskrit and *Prakrit* Calcutta..

it has pleased a gracious Providence to link the destinies of India with those of England, Sanskrit learning has acquired a new importance. In order that England may rightly understand India, she must study the latter in the wisdom and learning of her saints and sages. The social economy of Hindu society precluding all free intercourse between the Englishman and the Hindu, the former by applying himself to the study of the Hindu scriptures, can frame to himself a genuine image of the mind and manner of the modern Hindu. The one thing needful is that the Englishman, representing our Gracious Sovereign, should attain an *insight* into the permanent traits of the national character. This knowledge is *essential*, and no acquaintance with the more details can dispense with the same. Nor in the face of the mighty force of the conservatism that sways the East, much weight need be attached to the plausible objection that the Sanskrit works refer to antiquity. Sir Monier Williams wrote wisely when he said, 'In India the lapse of centuries cannot effect radical changes in the character of the inhabitants.' For an instance of the national resistibility to change witness the slender radical alteration these many years of English rule have effected in the constitution of the Hindu national character. From considerations like these, it will be evident that the task on which we intend to enter, is very important. The time, we fancy, has arrived when an organized and steady endeavour should be made for lighting up the dark regions of the distant Past pertaining to the Hindus of ancient India. Now that the barbarous theory of 'The people for the Prince', has been superseded by the Divine theory of 'The Prince for the people',[105] and England seriously intends making her rule a blessing to the children of the soil, it is more

---

[105] Manmatha Nath Dutt may not have actually read a translation of Nicholas Machiavelli's *Prince*. But if he did read a translation, it would probably have been the 1640 Edward Dacres translation.

> than ever incumbent on Englishmen to enter into the spirit of the nation's nature and idiosyncrasies—and the best, if not the sole way, of doing so, is to study the great treatises treasuring up in hieroglyphic characters the wisdom and culture of the gymnosophists of India.

The trail of correspondence, buried in the files, makes it clear that the Valmiki Ramayana translation was Manmatha Nath Dutt's first translation from Sanskrit to English. To refresh our memories, the first six *kandas* of the Valmiki Ramayana translation were published in 1891, by Deva Press. The *Uttara Kanda* followed in 1894. By that time, Elysium Press had been set up. *Gleanings from the Indian Classics*, Vol. I was also published by Deva Press. Thus, Elysium Press was set up in late 1893 or early 1894. The prospectus clearly tells us that *The Wealth of India* was started in July 1892. At the time of the Valmiki Ramayana translation, there is nothing to suggest the existence of the society either. How was the venture of publishing the Valmiki Ramayana managed? We have the answer in Manmatha Nath Dutt's own words. He says:

> Some years after the first publication of the English translation of the *Mahabharata*,[106] I undertook the publication of the English translation of its sister-work, namely, *Ramayana*. I have the greatest pleasure to announce that without much Government patronage I have been able to bring this work to a successful completion, depending entirely on general subscription and sale. Nearly five thousand English *Ramayana* have been sold at Rs 16 each, and in a business point of view it might be considered a great success.

Those who bought copies of the *Ramayana* were called patrons and we have some of their names.[107]

---

[106] The Mahabharata translation refers to the Ganguli one, not the Dutt one.

[107] We have retained the spellings from the prospectus, apart from correcting a few minor

- Government of Bengal[108]
- Government of North Western Provinces
- Government of Madras
- Government of Ceylon
- Text Book Committee of Punjab
- Director of Public Instruction, Berar
- Administrator of Porbundur Estate
- Tributary Chief of Raja Nangaon[109]
- Honourable Maharaja of Natore
- Tributary Chief Mahendra of Orissa[110]
- Raja of Kessengunj
- Theosophical Society
- Maharaja of Mysore
- Maharaja of Ulwar
- Maharaja of Travancore
- Raja of Ramnud
- Holkar of Indore
- Maharaja of Cashmere
- Rao of Cutch
- Raja of Cochin
- Gaekwar of Baroda
- Thakore Shaheb of Bhavnagar
- Thakore Shaheb of Palitana
- Thakore Shaheb of Gondal
- Thakore Shaheb of Limbdi

typos.

108 Government patronage, as mentioned in the quote above, only meant the government bought some copies, nothing more than that.

109 This refers to the Princely State of Raj Nandgaon.

110 Shura Pratap Singh Dev Mahendra of Dhenkanal.

- Nawah Bahadur of Junagad
- Maharajah of Benares
- Maharajah of Hutwa
- Maharajah of Kolapur
- Maharajah of Dhar
- Rajah of Rutlam
- Jam Shaheb of Navnagar
- Thakore Shaheb of Drangadra
- Maharajah of Burdwan
- Maharajah of Dumraon
- Maharajah of Nagpur
- Nawab Bahadur of Murshidabad
- Nawab of Bhawalpur
- Thakore Shaheb of Wala
- Samrat Singji of Pulitana[111]
- Maharajah of Vijianagram
- First Prince of Travancore
- Second Prince of Travancore
- Senior Consort of Travancore
- Junior Consort of Travancore
- Raja Nowloji Rao of Nagpur
- Sir Dinshaw M. Petit
- Rai Yatindra Nath Chowdhury, Zemindar of Taki
- Kumar Manmatha Nath Mitter, Jhamapukur
- Kumar Brojendra Kissore Rai Chowdhuri, Maimensing
- Kumar Indra Chundra Singh
- Byramji Jijibhoy
- Moharajah Sir Jotindra Mohan Tagore Bahadur

[111] Kathiwada Princely State.

- Raja Surja Kanta Acharjia Bahadur[112]
- Raja Narendra Lall Khan Bahadur, Narajole
- Maharaja Sir Narendra Krishna[113]
- Babu Chundy Lall Singhi
- Babu Guru Prosunno Ghose
- Babu Kali Kissen Tagore
- Haridas Beharidas, Zemindar of Nariad[114]
- B.K. Mehta of Bhownagore
- V.G. Oza of Bhownagore
- Lalubhoy Shamuldas of Bhownagore
- Dewan Bahadur Manibhoi Joshibhoy of Baroda
- Dewan Bahadur Lakshman Ganganath of Baroda
- Dewan Regent of Pudukota, Madras
- Zeminder of Puleanpote, Madras
- Zeminder of Palavanathan, Madras
- Right Honourable Lord Harris[115]
- Right Honourable Lord Reary[116]
- Right Honourable Lord Ripon
- Honourable Sir J.B. Lyall[117]
- Honourable Sir Charles Elliott[118]
- Honourable W.J. Woodburn[119]

---

[112] Worth noting, also from Mymensingh.

[113] Narendra Krishna Deb from the Sovabazar Raj family.

[114] This probably means Nadiad.

[115] This must be George Robert Canning Harris, Governor of Bombay.

[116] This is probably a typo and should read Lord Reay, Donald James Mackay, Governor of Bombay before Lord Harris.

[117] James Broadwood Lyall. At the time, he would have been the Lieutenant Governor of Punjab.

[118] Member of the Governor General's Council.

[119] This must mean John Woodburn, Lieutenant Governor of Bengal. So the 'W' is a typo.

- Sir Alexander Mackengie, Bengal[120]
- Honourable A.R. Scoble[121]
- Honourable Sir P.P. Hutchins[122]
- Lieutenant Colonel A.W. Baird, Mint Master
- Honourable Sir Comer Petheram[123]
- Honourable Sir John Edge[124]
- Honourable Justice J.F. Norris
- Honourable Justice L.R. Tottenham
- Honourable Justice J.O. Pigot
- Honourable Justice H.C. Hill
- Honourable Justice W. Macpherson
- Honourable Justice H.W. Gordon
- Honourable Justice Guru Das Banerjee
- Honourable Justice Chunder Madhab Ghose
- Honourable Justice Mr Parson
- Honourable Justice Farran
- Honourable Justice R.G. Ranade
- Honourable Sir Alfred Croft[125]
- Honourable J.M. Chitnavis
- Raja Mohimaranjan Rai Chawdhuri, Kakina
- Honourable Sir David Barbour[126]
- E.A. De Brett, Assistant Commissioner, Bilaspur
- Raja Rameshwar Mallia Bahadur
- Raja Runjit Singh Bahadur, Nasipur

---

[120] Alexander Mackenzie, Chief Commissioner of Burma.

[121] Member of the Governor General's Council.

[122] Member of the Governor General's Council.

[123] At the time, Chief Justice of Calcutta High Court.

[124] At the time, Chief Justice of the North Western Provinces.

[125] At the time, Director of Public Instruction, Bengal.

[126] Finance Member of the Governor General's Council.

- Maharaja of Tipperah
- F.T. Handley
- Raja of Bhinga
- Raja Vaidyanath Pandit Bahadur, Cuttack
- Colonel J.G. Forbes
- A. Smith
- H.J.S. Cotton
- F.M. Haliday
- H. Lee
- T.C. Harrison
- E. F. Pargiter
- T.W. Richardson
- T. Wilcox
- E.C. Ozanne
- John Dyson
- A. Fuhrer
- H.C. Streetfield
- R.C. Dutt
- J. Tweedy
- Major W.B. Ferris
- Captain Saddler
- H.T. Aston of Ahmedabad
- Dr Sterin of Lahore
- C.C. Stevens
- W.C. Bolton
- H. Luson
- F.H. Skrine
- P.H. Obrien
- J.L. Lea
- G.A. Gierson

- E.H. Blakesby
- R.A. Gamble
- Colonel H.R. Thuillier
- Surgeon Major W.H. Gregg
- Surgeon Major D.D. Cunningham
- Surgeon Major D.O.C. Raye
- Surgeon Major R.C. Saunders
- W.O. Bell Irving
- C.H. Moore
- J.L. Mackay
- R. Steel
- H.B.H. Turner
- S.E.J. Clarke
- E. Trelawney
- Right Reverend Lord Bishop of Calcutta
- His Grace, the Most Reverend Paul Goethals

Geographically, and cutting across slices of society, this listing of 'patrons' is nothing short of impressive. What exactly was a patron? We get an idea from what Manmatha Nath Dutt planned to do with the Mahabharata.

> I am printing five thousand copies at present to avoid all risk, for I can safely calculate and depend on the patronage of about three thousands of my *Ramayana* subscribers whom I claim as my personal friends, for I and my Managing Agent have seen almost all of them and they have subscribed to all my works. Therefore I might safely say that I incur no risk, for I am certain of three thousand subscribers whose subscriptions will cover all the expenses of printing.

This means a patron paid the sum of Rs 16 upfront and the translator/publisher was assured of a market of 3,000. As early subscribers, patrons also obtained a discount on the printed price.

I have mentioned a correspondence with the government that started in April 1890. The early correspondence is lost, but we can gather its gist from the notings in the subsequent files.

> In March 1890 Babu Manmatha Nath Datta submitted an application soliciting the patronage of the Government of India to an English translation of Valmiki's Ramayana in Sanskrit. The application was referred to the Government of Bengal for opinion of Mr Tawney on the translation. It was further enquired whether His Honor proposed to give any assistance to the project. The Government of Bengal in reply forwarded a copy of a letter from the Director of Public Instruction submitting the opinion of Mr Tawney and Professor Nilmani Mukerjea. It was stated that a strong case had not been made out for Government support. Babu Manmatha Nath Dutt was informed accordingly.

The 'Mr Tawney' in question was Charles Henry Tawney, who was himself a great translator from Sanskrit to English. At the time, he was the principal of Presidency College and had already translated *Kalidasa*, *Bhavabhuti*, *Bhartihari* and *Somadeva* from Sanskrit to English. Nilmani Mukerjea/Nilmani Mukhopadhyaya was Professor of Sanskrit in Presidency College. For Bibliotheca Indica, this was precisely the time when he was editing the *Kurma Purana* in Sanskrit. Note that the Director of Public Instruction, Bengal, was one of the patrons for the Valmiki Ramayana. Note that nothing had been said about quality. A strong case had not been made out for government support. What did government support mean? No grant or subsidy was intended. As the file notings show, what was intended was 'support by the purchase of copies for distribution to schools and colleges' and nothing more. Had Manmatha Nath Dutt studied in Presidency College, might the principal and professor of Presidency College been kinder? One shouldn't be unfair, but Manmatha Nath

Dutt did study in Scottish Church College.

As we have remarked earlier, the introduction to the translation of the Valmiki Ramayana was not replicated in subsequent translations. The quality of the Ramayana translation was superior to some of what came later. The reviews of the Ramayana translation were rather good. Here is a sample, reproduced in the prospectus mentioned earlier.

> *People's Friend* (Madras): 'The Ramayana under the able hands of Mr. Dutt will take a place among the English classics.'
>
> *Bangabashi* (Calcutta): 'Babu Manmatha Nath Dutt, M.A., Rector of the Kesub Academy, has already won reputation by his English Translation of the Ramayana [...] His Ramayana is a proof of the mastery of English style he has acquired.'
>
> *New India* (Calcutta): 'Babu Manmatha Nath Dutt has already made his mark in the world of literature as the translator of the Ramayana.'
>
> *Times of Assam:* 'His translation of the "Ramayana" has been spoken of highly in all quarters, both as evincing great mastery of English style as well as being a faithful and correct rendering of the original.'
>
> *Englishman:* 'The translation of "Ramayana" procured for Mr. Dutt the honour of election as a member of the Royal Asiatic Society.'

If *Englishman* was right, and there is no reason why it should not have been, we have an explanation for the MRAS.

Unfortunately, after this success, in my view, things took a turn for the worse and Manmatha Nath Dutt could get this reversed only around 1900, or thereabouts. Despite this, some of the perception stuck. From a translator, which was his USP, Manmatha Nath Dutt turned into a businessman and entrepreneur. This was all fine, as long as his basic USP did not get diluted. Sadly, he overstretched himself and this did cause the dilution.

After the Ramayana translation, *The Wealth of India* was launched in July 1892. The society was established, and Elysium Press too was also set up.

> The object of this series is to undertake the publication of the standard Sanskrit works and to place them within the easy reach of all English-knowing people. It will be regularly issued in monthly parts of six forms each, demy, octavo, and in such an order that each work on completion may be bound up into a separate book.

Such was the announcement that *The Wealth of India* made, along with a promise of a time frame of 10 years, within which, eight translations would be completed. These were: (*i*) *Bhagavata Purana*; (*ii*) *Vishnu Purana*; (*iii*) *Agni Purana*; (*iv*) *Garuda Purana*; (*v*) *Markandeya Purana*; (*vi*) *Kamandakiya Nitisara*; (*vii*) *Mahanirvana Tantra* and (*viii*) *Harivamsha*. These would be sold for Rs 16, Rs 6, Rs 10, Rs 10, Rs 5, Rs 5, Rs 10 and Rs 10, respectively, and added up to a total of Rs 72. However, if you subscribed to the entire series, as long as you were a resident of India, erstwhile Ceylon or erstwhile Burma, the cost would be reduced to Rs 50. This was a good deal, provided Manmatha Nath Dutt could maintain the quality, while sticking to the timeline he had proposed. In addition to the eight listed translations, there was also the *Gleanings from the Indian Classics* series that had to be accommodated into the time frame. There will be more on this subject in Chapter 6. On top of these, there was the Mahabharata. Something had to give. Manmatha Nath Dutt compromised on quality. He became a bookseller and publisher, moving away from the role of translator of his Ramayana days. Let me repeat a quote I gave earlier, because the purport may have been missed.

> I am printing five thousand copies at present to avoid all risk, for I can safely calculate and depend on the patronage of about three thousands of my Ramayana subscribers whom I claim as my personal friends, for I and my Managing Agent have seen almost all of them and they have subscribed to all my works.

Where did the managing agent come from? Indeed, why was a managing agent needed? As long as Deva Press was the publisher, the responsibility for copyediting and proofreading was largely someone else's. With Elysium Press being set up, Manmatha Nath Dutt assumed that responsibility too. He did a sloppy job in that and he did a sloppy job in the translation too. For the Mahabharata translation, he freely borrowed from Ganguli. For the *Vishnu Purana* translation, he freely borrowed from Wilson. For the *Markandeya Purana*, he freely borrowed from Pargiter. The damage was done. By extrapolation, the merits of the *Agni Purana*, *Garuda Purana*, *Kamandakiya Nitisara* and *Mahanirvana Tantra* translations were discounted. As part of the Bibliotheca Indica Series, Ramnarayana Vidyaratna and Rajendralal Mitra published an edited Sanskrit version of *Kamandakiya Nitisara* in 1884. However, for a very long time, Manmatha Nath Dutt's translation remained the only translation in English.[127] Manmatha Nath Dutt diluted the quality not only by borrowing, but also in another way. To quote him on his forthcoming Mahabharata translation: 'The translation of the work has been undertaken not only by myself, but by some of my friends and co-workers, gentlemen whom I have considered to be proper persons to undertake the task.' As far as one can make out, the Ramayana translation was done by him alone. However, as the burden of work increased, the translation work was delegated and outsourced, with imperfect supervision.

---

[127] An English translation (by Sisir Kumar Mitra) was brought out by Asiatic Society in 1982. This was a reprint (with the English translation) of Rajendralala Mitra, *The Nitisara or the Elements of Polity by Kamandaki*, Bibliotheca Indica.

The success of the Ganguli translation no doubt altered his perspective. To quote him again:

> Some fifteen years ago, the late Babu Protapa Chandra Rai[128] of Calcutta undertook the publication of an English translation of this great work and received patronage from the Government and from many of the Native Chiefs in India [...] It is a gigantic work, and the Government very properly bestowed upon him, as he well deserved, the Companionship of the distinguished Order of the Indian Empire.

On the Ganguli translation, here is a quote from P. Lal's annotated Mahabharata bibliography: 'This complete and faithful translation—the first of the two complete renderings into English of the epic and the only edition now available—is the monumental accomplishment strangely referred to, by scholars and bibliographers alike, as 'the P.C. Roy translation'.[129]

P.C. Roy, or Pratap Chandra Roy, was born in the village of Shanko in the Burdwan district of Bengal on 15 March 1842. When he grew up, he became a bookseller in Calcutta. By 1869 he had put by enough money to buy a small printing press and start a publishing concern. By the end of 1876 he had brought out a complete Bengali translation of the Mahabharata. Then a new idea fired him: the complete Mahabharata in English. His purpose was to unfold the richness of the Indian heritage to the British rulers and to foreigners in general; as his widow innocently explained in her epilogue, attached to the last book in 1896, 'If a knowledge of the mind of the people is of value to the administration of the country, who will deny the utility of an English translation of the Mahabharata to the British Government of India?' He knew his own English was not good enough; and his work at the press kept

---

[128] Pratap Chandra Roy was made Commander of Indian Empire (CIE).

[129] Lal, *An Annotated Mahabharata Bibliography.*

him too busy anyway. Luck brought him in touch with Babu Kisari Mohan Ganguli, a man with a brilliant academic record in English; Ganguli was entrusted with the work of translating the epic while Roy went around collecting funds from 'peasants and princes, Anglo-Indian officials and English and American sympathisers to warrant him in going forward'.[130] This was because his real ambition was to distribute the translated volumes free of cost—a task at which he eventually succeeded.

When his first wife died, P.C. Roy remarried in 1886. In 1889, he was made a Companion of the Order of the British Empire by Queen Victoria. He died of an undiagnosed illness on 10 January 1895. His will stated that his property be sold and the money from the sale be employed for three purposes—the completion of the English Mahabharata, the erection of a temple to Lord Shiva in his village and the construction of a tank there for the use of villagers. Babu Kisari Mohan Ganguli, who 'like a literary Atlas bore the heavy burden of the translation', and was acknowledged only in the last volume of the English translation. Though he had no hand at all in the translation, P.C. Roy put down his own name on the title page of the first nine volumes. The ambiguity that transformed a publisher into a translator and left K.M. Ganguli's glory unsung has, to my knowledge, been spotted only by Ronald Inden and Maureen Patterson, compilers of the University of Chicago's Bibliography to South Asian Studies; by K.M. Knott in the Janus Press Edition of the first two books of the Mahabharata and by A.C. Macdonnell in his *History of Sanskrit Literature*, where the translation has been

---

[130] Manmatha Nath Dutt reiterates that the Ganguli Mahabharata was sold for Rs 50. His intention was to bring out a cheaper edition. However, his ambition of distributing it free didn't work out.

> Babu Protapa's *Mahabharata* is a work beyond the means of the general public, its price being Rs. 50. And again a limited number of copies is being struck off and there is no chance of its ever being reprinted. Therefore a popular edition of an English translation of *Mahabharata* might be reasonably and safely floated in the market.

listed in the bibliography as having published at 'the expense of P.C. Roy' (it was surely at K.M. Ganguly's expense!). The 'utility' was quickly noticed. Lord Dufferin sanctioned a grant of ₹11,000 (whose purchasing power today would be around $20,000) and Lord Ripon gave 'a handsome contribution'. Sir Rivers Thompson 'was pleased to sanction a grant of ₹5,000; Sir Auckland Colvin gave ₹2,000 when he was appointed as Lieutenant-General of North West Provinces; Sir Alfred Croft granted ₹5,000.' The official list is augmented with American scholars and benefactors, such as Professor Lanman, Professor Maurice Bloomfield of Hopkins University, and others. K.M. Ganguli's translation was entirely a labour of love. 'My husband scarcely exaggerated the truth', wrote P.C. Roy's widow, 'when he used to say that [...] he was only the hand that did the work while Babu Kisari Mohan was the head that directed it. While lying on his death bed, he earnestly appealed to Babu Kisari Mohan to complete the undertaking. With tears in his eyes, Babu Kisari Mohan readily gave the assurance that was solicited, saying that he would not, on any account, give up the work.' At the end of the Mahabharata, Vol. XI (1896), Ganguli explains in his translator's postscript, 'Roy was against anonymity. I was for it.' He was afraid no one person could finish 'the whole of the gigantic work. It was, accordingly, resolved to withhold the name of the translator.' But hardly a fourth of the work had been accomplished when 'an influential Indian journal came down upon poor Pratap Chandra Roy and accused him openly of being a party to a great literary imposture'—that of posing as 'the translator of Vyasa's work, when, in fact, he was only the publisher.' Ganguli continues: 'Now that the translation has been completed, there can be no longer any reason for withholding the name of the translator. The entire translation is practically the work of one hand. Charu Chandra Mookherjee helped with portions of the Adi Parva and Sabha Parvas. About four forms of the Sabha parva were done by Professor Krishna Kamal Bhattacharya.'

Lal quoted Ganguli from Ganguli's translator's preface. A little bit of the sentence is missing in what Lal quoted:

> About four forms of the Sabha Parva were done by Professor Krishna Kamal Bhattacharya, and about half a fasciculus during my illness, was done by another hand. I should however state that before passing to the printer the copy received from these gentlemen I carefully compared every sentence with the original, making such alterations as were needed for securing a uniformity of style with the rest of the work.

He further adds:

> I should express my particular obligations to Pundit Ram Nath Tarkaratna, the author of 'Vasudeva Vijayam' and other poems, Pundit Shyama Charan Kaviratna, the learned editor of Kavyaprakasha with the commentary of Professor Mahesh Chandra Nyayaratna, and Babu Aghore Nath Banerjee, the manager of the Bharata Karyalaya. All these scholars were my referees on all points of difficulty. Pundit Ram Nath's solid scholarship is known to them that have come in contact with him. I never referred to him a difficulty that he could not clear up. Unfortunately, he was not always at hand to consult. Pundit Shyama Charan Kaviratna, during my residence at Seebpore, assisted me in going over the Mokshadharma sections of the Santi Parva. Unostentatious in the extreme, Kaviratna is truly the type of a learned Brahman of ancient India. Babu Aghore Nath Banerjee also has from time to time, rendered me valuable assistance in clearing my difficulties.

There are three points to note. First, for the Roy–Ganguli translation, there was an outright grant from the government, going beyond the mere purchase of a certain number of copies. Second, even when Ganguli delegated responsibility to others to do some of the translation, the final filter vested with him. Manmatha Nath Dutt was not that careful about consistency and quality. Third, for help with interpretations, Ganguli consulted Sanskrit pundits. There is no evidence that Manmatha Nath Dutt ever did this.

We know a little bit more about the Ganguli translation from a book published in 1897. It reads:

> The first complete translation of the poem was projected by Babu Pratap Chandra Rai, C.I.E. As a bookseller he had published a Bengali translation of the Mahabharata, which may have led the late Dr Rost to suggest to him the idea of an English translation. The expense was estimated at a lakh of rupees. An institution, to meet this outlay, was founded called the *Datavya Bharat Karyalaya*, and donations were asked from Government, Indian princes and others, it being proposed to distribute the bulk of the copies gratuitously. The first section was issued in 1883. On December 31, 1894, when the Thirteenth Book had been completed, the Babu bade farewell to his supporters, and, not long afterwards, he died. His widow, Sundara Bala Roy, then bravely took up the work. In a notice prefixed to the Mausala Parva, issued in 1896, she says: 'Assisted by his friends and patrons, my husband was able to issue 94 fascicules. Since his demise I have been able to issue 4 fascicules within a period of eight months. I have unhesitatingly devoted my little *stridhan* to the purpose, not only has that little been swallowed up, but I have been obliged to supplement it by debts.' In a notice, dated July 16, 1896, Sundari Bai [*sic*] announced the completion of the work, and rendered warm thanks to the friends who had assisted in the enterprise. Babu Pratap Chandra Rai claimed only to be the publisher of the work. The actual translator was Pandit Kesari Mohan Gauguli. In the first half of the work he generally adhered to the Bengal text; in the latter half to the Bombay edition. A memorial, signed by Sir Arthur Arnold, Professor Cowell, Sir M. Monier-

> Williams, Lord Northbrook, and others was lately presented to the First Lord of the Treasury applying for a pension to the Pandit who had laboured in the translation for thirteen years, and was now old. This monumental work reflects great credit both upon the translator, the publisher, and his widow. The translation contains in all about 7400 demy octavo pages, equal to nearly 25 volumes, each containing 500 pages. Another English translation, edited and published by Manmatha Nath Dutt, M.A., Rector, Keshub Academy, was commenced in 1895. It has been printed as far as the Bhishma Parva.[131]

Attempting to be Pratap Chandra Roy and Kisari Mohan Ganguli rolled into one, Manmatha Nath Dutt also sought to replicate the revenue model for the Roy–Ganguli venture, but with less success.

As I have said before, in March 1890, Manmatha Nath Dutt wrote to the government of India, soliciting patronage for the Ramayana translation. He wrote again on 5 February 1896, to Honourable J. Woodburn, who was then Home Member of the Viceregal Council. The address was 65/2 Beadon Street and a copy of the letter has been kept in the Home Department records.

> I have the honor[132] to forward herewith one copy of the first volume of Srimadbhagavatam forming a portion of a series of translations called *The Wealth of India* the publication of which I have taken in hand. The object of this series is to bring out the translations of eight standard Sanskrit works and to place them within the easy reach of [the] English knowing public. I have been working on this work for the last three years and within

---

131 *Epic Poems and Puranas, The Sacred Books of the East, Described and Examined; Hindu series*, Vol.3, Christian Literature Society for India, India, London and Madras, 1898.

132 Note the spelling of 'honor' in this and the subsequent letter. Also, this was the beginning of a period when technology increasingly switched from reed pens to fountain pens, but fountain pens were still a rarity. The notings in the government files were clearly done with reed pens. However, both of Manmatha Nath Dutt's letters seem to have been written with fountain pens, a very unusual occurrence.

> this time one book namely Vishnupuranam has been finished and Srimadbhagavatam is well-nigh complete. The completion of the remaining six books will extend over seven years more. The price for the whole set of eight works including postage is either Rupees fifty or Rupees six per annum. I beg also to send the first book of the English Translation of the Mahabharata which I have taken up for the people. The price for the entire work is Rs 12/- twelve including postage in advance. The first two books are out and the whole work is likely to be completed within two years. Considering the bulk of the work I might say that this is the cheapest publication ever taken in hand. Up to this time the publications of this nature have been priced so enormously that their circulation has been more or less confined to a limited few. People, having taste and not the means, have not been able to purchase them. My humble attempt is to remove this difficulty and to make these works more popular. But even now there is not such a demand for these works as to meet all expenses of publication out of the proceeds of sale. I have got therefore, Sir, to seek the patronage of my country's Government. I humbly pray that you will be pleased to grant me such a substantial help as you may think proper. I beg to enclose herewith a copy of the Prospectus. I have the honor to be Honorable Sir, Your most obedient servant.

The letter was signed Manmatha Nath Dutt, 'Editor and Publisher'. The description did not say translator, highlighting the Dutt dilemma mentioned earlier. Consider from a translator's perspective the eight texts promised in *The Wealth of India*, namely (*i*) *Bhagavata Purana*; (*ii*) *Vishnu Purana*; (*iii*) *Agni Purana*; (*iv*) *Garuda Purana*; (*v*) *Markandeya Purana*; (*vi*) *Kamandakiya Nitisara*; (*vii*) *Mahanirvana Tantra* and (*viii*) *Harivamsha*.

Any objective advice to a translator would have something like the following. Don't attempt a translation of *Vishnu Purana*, Wilson has done it. Don't attempt a translation of *Markandeya Purana*, Pargiter has done it. And to bring in the Mahabharata, don't attempt it, Ganguli has done it. (Ganguli did not translate *Harivamsha*.) Attempt these only if you are going to do a better job. In any event, there are other texts waiting to be translated. However, as a publisher and owner of Elysium Press, Manmatha Nath Dutt was tempted by a possible market for cheaper versions. Since the 'demand for these works' was uncertain, he was also tempted by the government grant given to Ganguli's Mahabharata. As we saw earlier, this wasn't a simple case of purchasing a certain number of books. There was an outright grant too. This was an era without stringent copyright legislations, and since he wished to reprint translations that had already been done, Manmatha Nath Dutt simply became an 'editor' and marginally altered the already translated works, aided by some 'friends and co-workers'.

What occurred thereafter was inevitable. The notings in the files were devastating, which also illustrate the broader dilemma the government faced. Although the name of the person who wrote this particular note is irrelevant for our purposes, this one was by A.T. Pringle.[133]

> Three books are forwarded. These are (1) the Vishnupuranam; (2) the Srimatbhagavata Puranam; (3) the Mahabharata. Only (1) is complete. As to (1), the translator states both on the title-page and in his preface that it is 'based on' Wilson's translation. This is honest, but considering the extent to which he has drawn on that work, it would have been more honest still not to have touched a wording of it. Comparing the two together, it is difficult to believe that there has been much, if any independent translation; at the beginning of the book, there is more show of departure from Wilson, but elsewhere sentence

[133] Assistant Secretary, Madras and Member of the Governor General's Council.

after sentence is taken from him, with just here and there needless verbal alterations, generally spoiling the English [...] It is difficult to open a page, and not find several mistakes[134] of a kind which, if a clerk made them, would prevent his advancement in an office [...] A very safe judge, the present Librarian of the India Office has told the Government that Babu Manmatha Datta has not acquired any reputation as a Sanskrit scholar, and that his translations are 'often grotesque and unintelligible without the original'. It may be concluded that as renderings of the Sanskrit originals, the present translations and those to come are and will be unscholarly, and where scholarship is wanting, a translator should at least be equipped with other qualifications, his English should be as good as that, say, of a Secretarial clerk, and if he is uncertain in spelling, he should be careful to have his proofs passed by somebody who is competent to correct mistakes such as those of which a few samples have just been given. But where this is no scholarship, where the translator either cannot write tolerably good English *throughout* a book, or does not take the trouble to revise the work of his assistants, and where there are no signs of care in editing, it is for consideration whether official assistance should be afforded. The difficulty is that such assistance cannot be given without creating a wrong impression: the mere fact that the Government of India have set down their names on a subscription list is in many quarters regarded as some guarantee of the worth of a book, and applications for support to Local Governments or to Native States have twice as many chances of success if it can be said in the prospectus that the Governor General in Council has taken some copies. And, again, it is perhaps well that there should be uniformity in the treatment of cases of this kind. The

[134] In 'composition and orthography'.

> grant of substantial help to the venture of the late Babu Pratap Chandra Rai was probably a grave error, and the idea of very large subscriptions to works undertaken by persons having no pretence to scholarship would not now be entertained. But if help is afforded in one case, it should be in another; if copies of these three books and others of the set are taken, the decision not to subscribe to Babu Sasi Mohun Datta's translation of the Bhagavata Purana[135] seems to be a little unfair: his work was worse edited in some respects than any of Babu Manmatha Datta's, but there were signs of misdirected endeavours to edit it well. Both authors were, it may be suspected, stimulated by the success of Babu Pratap Chandra Rai's monster work. On the whole, considering how little direct pecuniary benefit there is to any translator in an order for four or five copies of a work, and how liable to misapprehension any action of the Government in this respect must be, I hesitate to recommend that any patronage should be extended on the present occasion.

Opinions had been sought from various people and on 28 May 1896, Alfred Croft, director of Public Instruction, Bengal, wrote to the secretary of the Government of Bengal:

> I have the honour to subjoin an extract from a letter N. 237 dated the 22 February 1895[136], from Mahamahopadhyaya Mahes Chandra Nyayaratna, C.I.E., the then Principal of Sanskrit College,[137] expressing his opinion on the English translation of Srimatbhagabata and Vishnupurana by Babu

---

135 This statement can be misinterpreted. The translator was Mohendra Nath Chatterjee. Sasi Mohan Datta was the publisher. The translation was published in Calcutta in 1895.

136 Since Manmatha Nath Dutt wrote in February 1896, this date is odd, suggesting that some earlier letter by Manmatha Nath Dutt is missing in the files. Perhaps that letter was written to the Government of Bengal and not to the Government of India, explaining why it is missing in the files.

137 This is circumstantial evidence suggesting 'Shastri' was not a studied degree through Sanskrit College, but an honourary one.

> Manmantha Nath Datta, M.A.: 'I do not consider the translations of *Shrimatbhagabata* and *Vishnupurana* published in "The Wealth of India" deserving of support for the purchase of copies for distribution to schools and colleges. The want of closeness and accuracy in the translations has, in my humble opinion, arisen from want of scholarship and not from there being variations in the text. I again compared the translations of several stanzas, taken at random from different parts of both the books and I am sorry to say that I found not a single stanza correctly rendered. In none of these cases is there any variation in the reading.' A similar opinion has been expressed by Babu Nilmani Mukherjea, M.A., the present Principal of the Sanskrit College, as to the merits of the English translation of Mahabharata by the same author. In view of these adverse criticisms I am unable to recommend the works for the support of Government.

That was that. On 30 June 1896, Manmatha Nath Dutt of 65/2 Beadon Street was informed:

> With reference to your letter of the 5 February last soliciting the patronage to a series of English translations of certain Sanskrit works, I am directed to inform you that the Government of India regret their inability to accede to your request. The books noted below which accompanied your letter are returned.

It didn't quite end there. On 19 August 1898, Manmatha Nath Dutt again wrote to the Viceroy and Governor General. The address continued to be 65/2 Beadon Street.

> Sir, I have the honor in sending you a copy of Kamandakiya Nitisara, the most celebrated work on Hindu Politics. I have taken much pains in collating the text and rendering it into English. My object in sending you this copy is to solicit the

patronage of His Excellency so that His Excellency may be pleased to encourage my undertaking by purchasing one or more copies which His Excellency may think proper. As a subject it is quite natural for me that I should look up for help to my rulers for popularizing the great Hindu literature. I have the honor to be Sir, Your most obedient servant.

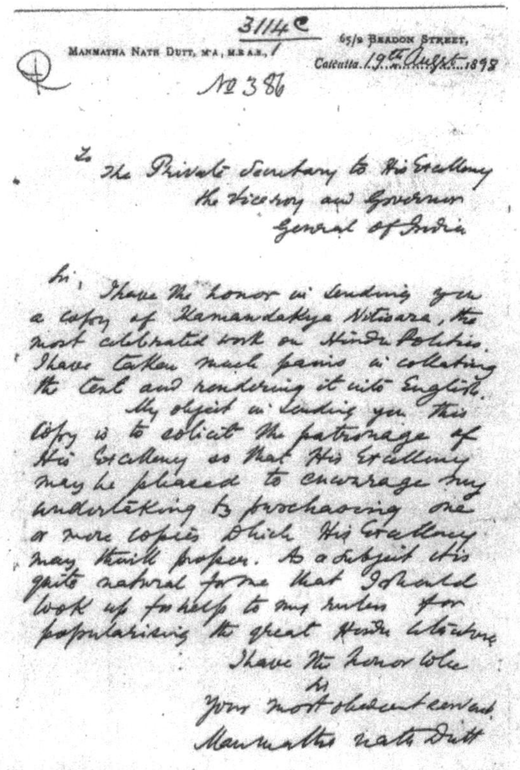

3114 C

MANMATHA NATH DUTT, M.A., M.R.A.S., / 65/2 BEADON STREET,
Calcutta. 19th August 1898

No 386

To The Private Secretary to His Excellency
the Viceroy and Governor
General of India

Sir, I have the honor in sending you a copy of Kamandakya Nitisara, the most celebrated work on Hindu Politics. I have taken much pains in collating the text and rendering it into English.
My object in sending you this copy is to solicit the patronage of His Excellency so that His Excellency may be pleased to encourage my undertaking by purchasing one or more copies which His Excellency may think proper. As a subject it is quite natural for me that I should look up for help to my rulers for popularising the great Hindu literature.

I have the honor to be
Sir
Your most obedient servant
Manmatha Nath Dutt

This time, he did not describe himself as editor and publisher, but one need not read too much into this. The earlier file notings were dug up and they diminished his credibility. The notings in the files were just as harsh, even more so.

> Babu Manmatha Nath Dutt is understood to be a most respectable and estimable person, but it is clear that he is a book-maker and that he is perfectly incompetent in several respects [...] The misspellings, instances of neglect to correct the blunders of the compositors, and so on, to which attention is drawn in this note, are of course trivial matters in one sense, and if it were known that the editor had any pretensions to be a real scholar in Sanskrit they might be pardoned. But they are I venture to think typical of this class of booksellers.

If our translator reduced himself to the status of a bookseller, it was his own doing. Accordingly, on 16 September 1896, the private secretary to the viceroy wrote to Manmatha Nath Dutt.

> I have laid before His Excellency the Viceroy your letter of the 19th Ultimo conveying the request that His Excellency would be pleased to purchase one or more copies of your version of the work entitled 'Kamandakiya Nitisara'. In reply I am desired to inform you that His Excellency regrets that he is unable to comply with your request.

The Home Department files have nothing more about Manmatha Nath Dutt. I have remarked earlier that the run of the mill Bengali *bhadralok* wouldn't have completed his MA degree in 1888 and started a society, a magazine and a publishing house in 1890. This probably had something to do with his father and uncle not having been classic Bengali zamindars. Perhaps, they made their fortune as entrepreneurs, as contractors for the railways, and bought their estates with that money.

SIX

BEYOND TRANSLATIONS

Manmatha Nath Dutt was more than a translator, editor and bookseller. It is worth repeating his society's objectives:

1. To undertake the publication of rare Sanskrit texts not published before.
2. To undertake the publication of cheap editions of texts already published.
3. To publish popular editions of works relating to the antiquity of Indian literature.
4. To publish such works of oriental scholars as have gone out of print.
5. To undertake translations of standard Sanskrit works into various living languages.

Of these, I have already highlighted publication of works of Oriental scholars and cheap editions of texts already published. There is only one single instance of publication of 'rare Sanskrit texts' that is left to tackle. Of the 16 *samhitas* that form the Dharmashastras, this is the only one (published in 1908) that is without an English translation. This 1908 volume only had Sanskrit text. 'We have followed the Bengal recension which is generally regarded as the most genuine and reliable.' The English translations, and a few more Sanskrit texts, were published in the second volume. This still leaves the translations and 'popular editions of works relating to the antiquity of Indian literature'.

If Manmatha Nath Dutt is remembered at all today, it is as a translator. And since the translations he is usually identified with are those of the Mahabharata, the *Vishnu Purana* and the *Markandeya Purana*, where he did draw on the work of others, it is often assumed that he exhibited no originality. As a general proposition, that is certainly not true. The Dharmashastra texts, *Agni Purana* and *Garuda Purana* are cases in point. Roughly at that time, some of the Dharmashastra texts were also being translated by George Bühler and Julius Jolly under the Sacred Books of the East series. Later, others were translated by Ganganath Jha and Pandurang Vaman Kane. In very recent times, Patrick Olivelle has translated a few more. However, all these translations are usually of the more important Dharmashastra texts. For the minor ones, the Manmatha Nath Dutt translations still remain the only translations in English. There is still no translation of the *Garuda Purana* in English other than his translation. A translation of the *Agni Purana* was recently brought out by N. Gangadharan.[138] Until the 1980s, Manmatha Nath Dutt's translation was the only English translation of the *Agni Purana*. Despite this, there was a tendency to be excessively harsh on him. His translation of the *Mahanirvana Tantra* was published in 1900. Arthur Avalon's translation of the *Mahanirvana Tantra* was published soon after, in 1913.[139] About his predecessor, Arthur Avalon said:

> Yet of all the forms of Hindu Shastra, the Tantra is that which is least known and understood, a circumstance in part due to the difficulties of its subject-matter and to the fact that the key to

[138] N. Gangadharan, *The Agni Purana*, Motilal Banarsidass, Delhi, 1984–87.

[139] Arthur Avalon, *The Great Liberation, Mahanirvana Tantra, Translation and Commentary*, Ganesh and Company, Madras, 1913.

> much of its terminology and method rest with the initiate. The present translation is, in fact, the first published in Europe of any Indian Tantra. An inaccurate version rendered in imperfect English was published in Calcutta by a Bengali editor some twelve years ago, preceded by an Introduction which displayed insufficient knowledge in respect of what it somewhat quaintly described as 'the mystical and superficially technical passages' of this Tantra [...] The translation published is that of the first part only. It is commonly thought [and was so stated by the author of the Calcutta edition in English to which I have referred] that the second portion is lost. This is, however, not so, though copies of the complete Tantra are rare enough.

Arthur Avalon was of course a pseudonym for John George Woodroffe (1865–1936), who prided himself on his knowledge of tantra.[140] His books on the subject did much to spread notions of tantra in the West. It is unlikely that Arthur Avalon did not know, or did not know of, Manmatha Nath Dutt. Consequently, it is a bit odd that Arthur Avalon did not even condescend to mention him by name, but simply dismissed him as 'a Bengali editor'. Others did not have as low an opinion as Arthur Avalon did. In 1902, after Manmatha Nath Dutt's translation of *Mahanirvana Tantra* was published in 1900, K.S. Macdonald wrote an essay on the Shakta religion.[141] Macdonald felt that Manmatha Nath Dutt's views were good enough to be quoted. He writes:

> Manmatha Nath Dutt (Shastri), M.A., M.R.A.S., Rector, Keshub Academy, and author of the 'Prose English Translation of the Mahanirvanam Tantram' and defender of the Tantric cult, contends that there is 'a great esoteric meaning behind

[140] The pseudonym was an allusion to King Arthur and the legendary island of Avalon.

[141] K.S. Macdonald, 'The Sakta Religion and the Female Sex', *The Calcutta Review*, Vol. CXV, July 1902.

> them'. 'All these', says Mr. Dutt, 'wine, meat, fish and women are objects of temptation. If a worshipper can overcome this temptation, the road to eternal bliss is clear for him.' Not so do the Tantras represent matters. These things are there according to the Tantras to be enjoyed alike as pleasing to the worshipper and to the worshipped.

Manmatha Nath Dutt was much more than a translator. In addition to translations, the corpus includes retelling stories (*Gleanings from the Indian Classics* Series), books on Hinduism (on Ayurveda, metaphysics and domestic duty), a book on the Buddha and a monograph on the Posta Raj. Since these have not been reprinted and are no longer readily accessible, it is worth explaining what they contain.

Published in 1900, *A Short Sketch of Posta Raj Family* is a monograph of 31 pages; it is not even a proper book. Towards the end of the seventeenth century, when the English moved from Hooghly to Sutanuti/Calcutta, Lakshmikanta Dhar, a member of the *subarna banik* community (a trading community that dealt primarily in gold) accompanied them. He was Lord Clive's banker and financially helped Clive in his fight against the Nawab. He continued to financially help the English in their wars against the Marathas. As a token of gratitude, the East India Company offered him, among other things, the title of 'Maharaja'. Lakshmikanta Dhar desired no such honour for himself. His daughter's son was Sukhomoy Roy and that honour was bestowed on him, the daughter's son. Among other things, Sukhomoy Roy built the road from Cuttack to Puri, so that pilgrims visiting the Jagannath temple in Puri could do so more easily. The word 'posta' means quay, embankment or jetty, and this was a jetty on the River Hooghly used by zamindars from Jorasanko. Most Bengalis have forgotten the history behind this term and remember the place only because of a nonsense rhyme written by Sukumar Ray! 'Shuntey pelum Posta giye, tomar naki meyer biye.'[142] Zamindars often commissioned such histories and Manmatha Nath Dutt was accordingly commissioned for a history of Posta Raj.[143] In the nineteenth century, the other great translator of the Mahabharata into English was Kisari Mohan Ganguli, a contemporary of Manmatha Nath Dutt. It is not widely known that, in similar vein, Kisari Mohan Ganguli was commissioned to do a brief history of the Andul Raj.

Despite it being a brief monograph, quite a bit of what is known about Posta Raj comes from Manmatha Nath Dutt.

> The Subarna Baniks are the Banker caste of Bengal. The members of this community are proverbially famous for their opulence. They trace their descent from Sonaka Adya, a Baisya, who migrated from Ramgarh in Ayodhya, many centuries ago, to the Court of Adisur, the then king of Bengal. The first seat of this caste still bears the name of *Subarnagram* or the golden village, so called in honor of the great gold merchant [...] When the English left Hughly to avoid the persecutions of the Mahomedans and settled further down the river in three of the most marshy and malarious villages that ever stood on the banks of the Ganges, a few native bankers shared their ill-fortune and followed them to these marshes, knowing full well with their usual shrewdness that trade and prosperity would flourish wherever the English would go [...] His Imperial Majesty the Emperor of Delhi, in appreciation of the loyal feelings and philanthropy of Maharaja Sukmoy Roy Bahadur, conferred on him the titled of Maharaja and gave him permission 'to command over four thousand men and

---

[142] 'I went to Posta and heard that your daughter is getting married.' My translation.

[143] A more comprehensive one was commissioned later. See, Benimadhub Chatterji, *A Short Sketch of Maharaja Sukhmoy Roy Bahadur and His Family*, Star Printing Works, Calcutta, 1929. This is a revised edition. The original edition was from 1910, shortly after Manmatha Nath Dutt did his version. The Dutt version must have been less than satisfactory.

> use a Palkie with fringes around it' in the fortieth year of His Majesty's reign.

Having disposed of Posta Raj, let's now turn to *Gleanings from the Indian Classics*. In this series, the prospectus promised the following:

> The object of undertaking the publication of this series is to place before the English-knowing public in a popular garb the most interesting and instructive mythological tales of India's literature—the characters of her heroes and heroines, prophets and sages etc. etc. It is beyond the possibility of any question that in India we have heroines, the like of whom we shall rarely find in any other literature. India is the mother of the superb Hinduism, the world-spreading Buddhism, and many other religions, which still have been shedding lustre upon the moral and intellectual character of humanity. We need not therefore say that her Prophets will be a very interesting study to the children of modern light and culture, especially at this period of high development of thought and science, when religion is being studied from the stands-points of science and history.

As promised in the prospectus, there would be four volumes of the *Gleanings from the Indian Classics*. The first volume was called 'Tales of Ind'. The second was 'Heroines of Ind'. The third volume would be on 'Prophets of Ind', specifically, Krishna and Buddha. The fourth and last volume was on other prophets, such as Chaitanya and Keshub. As published, *Gleanings from the Indian Classics*, Vol. IV has simply vanished. As we shall see, when it was published, the third volume did include some other prophets, but there was no Chaitanya and no Keshub. As I have said earlier, Manmatha Nath Dutt was associated with that branch of the Brahmo Samaj that was identified, after the schism, with Keshub Chandra Sen. It is fair to suggest that this branch became increasingly irrelevant. Did Manmatha Nath Dutt become increasingly disillusioned with the Brahmo Samaj?

The first book of the *Gleanings from the Indian Classics* series was published in 1893, with the added title of 'Tales of Ind'. This contained retellings of 17 stories, with two explanatory appendices on the Bhagavad Gita and yoga. Using the spellings of proper names used by Manmatha Nath Dutt, these 17 stories were on (*i*) battles of gods and demons; (*ii*) Shiva and Sati; (*iii*) Srikrishna; (*iv*) the monkey war; (*v*) the battle of Kurukshetra; (*vi*) Nala and Damayanti; (*vii*) Sribatsa and Chinta; (*viii*) Prahlada; (*ix*) the lost ring; (*x*) the boy devotee; (*xi*) Sabitri and Satyavan; (*xii*) Debjani; (*xiii*) Bilwamangala; (*xiv*) Harishchandra; (*xv*) Parasurama; (*xvi*) Bishaya and (*xvii*) the danava king. The monkey war refers to the story of the Ramayana, the lost ring is the story of Shakuntala, the boy devotee is about Dhruva and the danava king is about Bali. Sribatsa (Srivatsa) and Chinta is a Bengali folk tale and might not be that well known outside of Bengal.[144] In this story, there is a dispute between Shani and Lakshmi about the superiority of one vis-à-vis the other. To resolve this, they ask a man named Sribatsa to adjudicate. When Sribatsa favours Lakshmi, Shani subjects Sribatsa and his wife, Chintamani, to various travails. Lal Behari Dey (1824–1892) compiled the folk tales of Bengal in 1883.[145] This compilation had the Sribatsa–Chintamani story under the title, 'The Evil Eye of Sani'. Thus, to reiterate, Manmatha Nath Dutt did not plagiarize, but it is obvious his version of Sribasta and Chinta drew upon Lal Behari Dey's retelling of this story. Bilwamangala (Bilvamangala) is of course the story of Bilvamangala, who was addicted to a courtesan, also known as Chintamani,[146] before he discovered the true objective of life. Bishaya (Vishaya) is the story of Vishaya and Chandrahasa, which occurs in many places, including

[144] In 1955, there was a fairly successful Bengali film by the name of *Sribatsa Chinta*.

[145] Lal Behari Dey, *Folk Tales of Bengal*, Macmillan and Company, 1883. The illustrated 1912 edition is more popular.

[146] These are two different women, both coincidentally named Chintamani.

the Mahabharata.[147] Manmatha Nath Dutt clearly wrote this book for a British audience, not an Indian one—indeed, not even for an Indian readership conversant with English. A few quotes from his footnotes will illustrate this.

> The tale of the battle of gods and demons is an allegorical account of the ever-lasting struggle of the elements, the struggle of Life and Death, the struggle of the *forces* of preservation and destruction, the battle of the good and the evil, that is continuing from the beginning of time [...] The Christians have Satan, a quite distinct being from God; but the Hindus say that He as *Vishnu* is *All-good* and He as *Shiva* is *All-evil* [...] They should also mark that the demons were the greatest favourites of *God* as *Shiva*.

On that same subject of battles between the gods and the demons, he writes: 'Readers should notice the similarity of this battle with that of Satan with the gods in the fields of heaven. Evidently either of the two must have borrowed from each other.'

He further writes:

> Again there is a great similarity of this tale with the tale of the Bible. *Shoma*'s enticement of the heavenly goddess[148] and the consequent loss of heaven looks almost like Satan's enticement of Eve and the loss of Paradise. Again here in this tale the heaven was regained by the birth of a son[149] of God *Shiva*, just as in the Bible, by the birth of Christ.

On Vedavyasa having Vidura as a son, Manmatha Nath Dutt writes: 'All through this tale readers would find laxity of the marriage system and want of female chastity. It is evident, in those days the morals in

[147] It is a popular story in Karnataka and features in Yakshagana.

[148] Brihaspati's wife, Tara.

[149] Kartikeya.

India were quite different from those that of the modern world.'

For Shakuntala, there was a comparison that others have also made. 'The readers should mark the similarity of Kalidasa's *Shakuntala* with Shakespear's *Miranda* (Tempest).' For Manmatha Nath Dutt, the idea of the comparison must have come from Bankim Chandra Chatterjee (Chattopadhyay). In 1875–76, Bankim Chandra wrote an essay (in Bengali) in a Bengali magazine known as *Bangadarshan*, comparing Shakuntala, Miranda and Desdemona. Rabindranath Tagore also wrote a comprehensive essay in 1907 titled 'Prachin Sahitya' which touched upon the same topic, but that appeared after *Gleanings from the Indian Classics*, Vol. I was published. In connection with Sabitri (Savitri) and Satyavana, Manmatha Nath Dutt writes: 'Evidently all this means that a chaste, faithful and loving wife is a goddess whom even Pluto does not touch.' Finally, 'The ceremony of holy-thread is a sort of Baptismal.' Today, there is little in the first volume to hold a reader's interest and the statements I have just quoted will cause many people to shudder. Indeed, there was no reason for it to have done particularly well in 1893 either.

However, contrary to what I have said, *Gleanings from the Indian Classics*, Vol. I did do well. In the second volume of the series, published in 1897, it was stated in the preface:

> We are very glad to say that our attempt to popularize Indian Classics has met with immense success. In the course of six months the first edition of our 'Tales of Ind' has been all sold. We have received encouragement from all sides. We, therefore, hasten to place a few more volumes of the 'Gleanings' before our readers.

Writers mature, their styles change. But between 1893 and 1897, it was almost as if Manmatha Nath Dutt was a changed person. This doesn't come across in the translations, but it does come across in Manmatha Nath Dutt's other writings. What changed? Sucheta Kriplani was born in 1908. Her mother, Prembala, was educated and married into an educated family. Prembala must have been at least 20 when Sucheta Kriplani was born. This means Prembala was born around 1888. After two of her younger brothers were born, Prembala's mother, Charubala, died. Therefore, Charubala probably died around 1891. The deaths of wives are known to change the lives of many men. Perhaps one does need to highlight that Manmatha Nath Dutt's translations and other writings started from 1891 onwards. There was nothing that dated to before this year, except that compilation of English poems. In passing, we know his children were brought up by his in-laws. After his wife's death, there were no family responsibilities. The deaths of wives, or other near and dear ones, often draw men towards religion. As religious movements go, Bengal was in a bit of a churn at the time. There was Christianity. There were men in Bengal who were drawn towards it, even to the extent of getting converted. Lal Behari Dey was one such example. Clearly, Manmatha Nath Dutt was conversant with Christian tenets and stories, and the Bible in particular, but there is no evidence that he was ever drawn towards it, beyond a point. There were the theosophists and the Dhole connection shows that Manmatha Nath Dutt knew the theosophists quite well. Hirendranath Dutta (1860–1942), the famous lawyer, philosopher, scholar and politician, was also a theosophist.[150] Born into the Hatkhola Dutta family, Hirendranath Dutta would have had very close family connections with Manmatha Nath Dutt, perhaps a cousin, had Manmatha Nath Dutt himself been from the Hatkhola lineage. But as we saw, Manmatha Nath Dutt was probably not from the Hatkhola lineage. More pertinently, there is no evidence that Manmatha Nath Dutt was ever drawn towards the theosophist movement. There was the Brahmo Samaj, a movement Manmatha Nath Dutt had close links with, courtesy his marriage, because he was rector of Keshub Academy and because

[150] In 1893, in a Bengali magazine known as *Sahitya*, Hirendranath Dutta wrote two essays comparing Kalidasa and Shakespeare. Before studying law, he studied English (BA/MA) in Presidency College.

of his friends and acquaintances. The Brahmo Samaj movement has been extensively documented. However, barring the Keshub Academy angle, Manmatha Nath Dutt's name doesn't figure anywhere in the history of this movement. This may certainly be because he was not important enough to be mentioned. Alternatively, and much more likely, he was not mentioned simply because he was not very active. He had been drawn towards the Brahmo Samaj movement and may even have become a member, but that's about it.

There was Ramakrishna Paramahansa (1836–1886) and there is extensive documentation of his disciples, of the sanyasi or non-sanyasi variety, and others who visited him. Manmatha Nath Dutt's name doesn't find a name in this extensive documentation either. The Ramakrishna Math was established in Baranagore in 1887, after Ramakrishna Paramahansa's death, and this brings us to Swami Vivekananda (1863–1902), another contemporary of Manmatha Nath Dutt's, perhaps even a classmate in college, or a couple of years his senior. Swami Vivekananda's addresses at the Parliament of the World's Religions in Chicago in 1893 made a great impression on Manmatha Nath Dutt. The third volume of the *Gleanings from the Indian Classics* was published in 1899 and in that, he wrote:

> It is better for us to quote the most excellent address delivered before the Parliament of Religions in Chicago by one who has not only read the Hindu *Shastras* through and through but who has realized the highest ideal of the religion of the great *Rishis*. Perhaps it is the best sketch of Hinduism that was ever written or told.

Suffice to say, after Swami Vivekananda in Chicago, Manmatha Nath Dutt seems to have rediscovered Hinduism and what he wrote thereafter was no longer directed at an exclusively British audience. Nor did he feel compelled to bring in Christian parallels, unlike in *Gleanings from the Indian Classics*, Vol. I. But oddly enough, in that quote, Swami Vivekananda is not mentioned by name. That would have been a natural thing to do. Was that because Manmatha Nath Dutt knew Narendranath Datta closely, as a classmate, or as a senior, in Scottish Church College, and this metamorphosis into Swami Vivekananda was not that easy to accept? Was it because of his Brahmo Samaj connections that even though he was attracted towards what Swami Vivekananda said, he found it difficult to acknowledge it? Though one should not speculate too much, not using Swami Vivekananda's name is more than a bit strange.

Gleanings from the Indian Classics, Vol. II was about heroines. In the introduction to this volume, Manmatha Nath Dutt writes:

> There were gems and jewels in India which were the wonders of the human race, but far more beautiful and far more precious than all this is the Hindu Wife. She is the purest of all the gems that have ever been found in any part of the world. A brief narrative, of the characters and careers of some of those that have been reckoned as heroines in the pages of history, those whose names have come down from generation to generation as the glorious productions of woman-hood and those whom the people of India adore, admire and cherish as the idols of their worship, will show that they were none but the Hindu wives.

There is a description of the home and the hearth and the wife as the mistress of the house. There is also a long section, in the eventuality of widowhood. On this subject, he writes:

> In the unknowable mystery of destiny she often becomes a widow, and widowhood is but another shade of the Hindu marriage. Her belief is that marriage is not for this world alone, but for eternity and her husband is her husband for ever-lasting time through innumerable births and deaths.

As a signatory to the remarriage petition, Kashinath Dutta might not have approved of this. Indeed, most Brahmos would have disagreed.

In passing, the description of a Hindu marriage in *Gleanings from the Indian Classics*, Vol. II is quite unlike anything Manmatha Nath Dutt would himself have gone through, when he married Charubala. It is also unlike anything any of his Brahmo friends would have gone through.

> The next great event in her life is her marriage. The sounds of music rise above the noise of the household; the elders are smoking with all the gravity of busy men and receiving the guests with all the grace of oriental courtesy. Boys and girls in their holy-day attire frisk about the door; they laugh, they chat, they run to see how far still is the bridegroom with his merry suite. There in the Zenana matrons bustle about, doing a thousand nameless things and maidens peep through the windows to catch the first glimpse of the happy bridegroom. He comes in the garb of an ascetic; a red silken cloth is round his body, the garlands of white flowers are round his neck, his forehead is painted with the fragrant sandal. He comes to perform a solemn religious ceremony—the gravest and the most serious event of his life. He has passed the day in worshipping gods and goddesses and the departed spirits of his dead forefathers. He has prayed for their blessings on him and on her whom he is going to marry. And she too has spent the night in religious devotions, fasting and doing naught which is holy and impure [...] Face to face they sit; the father gives away his dearly loved child to his son-in-law and he accepts the precious gift. The reverend priest unites their hands and places round their necks the garlands of flowers, chains too strong to be ever broken. Fire is ablaze, incense is burnt, gods and goddesses are invoked; and fire, water, wind, ether and all the elements are called to be witnesses [...] Her childish hand trembles like an aspen leaf and her heart beats as if it would burst. [Later on,] at last the special day for entertaining sons-in-

law—the celebrated Hindu festival of *Jamai Shasti*—comes.

The Special Marriages Act was passed in 1872. As someone who identified with the Keshub Chandra Sen side of the Brahmo Samaj and who married Charubala, a woman from a family that also strongly identified with the Keshub Chandra Sen side of the Brahmo Samaj, Manmatha Nath Dutt and Charubala are certain to have been married under the Special Marriage Act. That's the reason something doesn't quite ring true—that is, his description is of a traditional Hindu marriage, with all its rituals. Indeed, it is the description of a traditional Hindu marriage in a rural Bengal setting, not that of urbanized and urbanizing Calcutta. Of course, Manmatha Nath Dutt need not have himself got married through Hindu rites for him to be able to describe such a marriage so vividly. He might have been from the bridegroom's party, such as the one that accompanies the groom to the wedding. He could have aldo been from the bride's side of the family. But, in either case, he would have had to experience the ceremony vividly enough for him to be able to describe it. However, I do want to emphasize the rural angle. Had Manmatha Nath Dutt been born in Calcutta and from the Hatkhola lineage, he wouldn't have had any direct experience of this, at least not under normal circumstances. Pabna was a completely different matter.

The descriptions of the heroines in *Gleanings from the Indian Classics*, Vol. II begin with Sati and Shiva and then go on to portray women from the Vedas and the Upanishads, before finally moving on to Lilavati (the mathematician) and Khana (the astrologer). After this, there are more contemporary women—Sanyukta (Prithviraj Chauhan's wife); Padmini, the Rani of Argal; Karum Devi (who was promised in marriage to the ruler of Mandore, but loved Sadoo, the daughter of a desert chief instead); Tara Bai (the wife of Prithviraj); Panna (the nursemaid to Uday Singh II of Mewar); Rani Durgavati (the queen of Ganore); the wife of Pratapaditya of Jessore; the wife of Jaswant Singh of Marwar (Queen of Jodhpur); Rani Bhabani (of

Natore); (Asamanya Jagat Seth's daughter); Devi Chaudhurani, the bandit lady; Ahalya Bai (of Indore); Princess Krishna (from Udaipur); Maharani Jhindan (Maharaja Duleep Singh's mother); the Rani of Jhansi and Mira Bai. From this listing, the influence of Lieutenant Colonel James Tod is obvious.[151] There was quite a bit of fascination in Bengal about Rajasthan. In fact, Romesh Chunder Dutt had not only translated the Ramayana and the Mahabharata into English in verse form, in 1878, he also published a book in Bengali titled *Rajput Jivan Sandhya*, with stories from Rajasthan.

A few of the stories in *Gleanings from the Indian Classics*, Vol. II are of course Bengal-specific. In one of the stories, we have Pratapaditya (1561–1611), a zamindar, and who later became the king of Jessore. Irrespective of what the real Pratapaditya was like, Bengali literature of the time portrayed him as a hero. When he wrote the story, there were three novels on Pratapaditya, one by Rabindranath Tagore.[152] Manmatha Nath Dutt probably got his idea from a novel written by Pratap Chandra Ghosh.[153] The plays on Pratapaditya came later, after Manmatha Nath Dutt had died. In another story, we have Rani Bhabani, who was a household name in Bengal because of her generosity and philanthropy. However, since Manmatha Nath Dutt mentioned both Rani Bhabani (1716–1795) and Ahalya Bai (1725–1795) of Indore, one suspects he might have been well-acquainted with Benaras (now known as Varanasi). After all, visitors, and even immigrants, from Bengal were fairly common in Benaras and Manmatha Nath Dutt could well have visited the city. Ahalya Bai wasn't that known in Bengal, at least not at the time. Of the two Durga temples in Benaras, one was built by Rani Bhabani,

[151] James Tod, *Annals and Antiquities of Rajast'han or the Central and Western Rajpoot States of India*, Vol. 1, 1829 and Vol. 2, 1832, London. These are the editions Manmatha Nath Dutt would have read, not the subsequent 1920 editions.

[152] The book by Tagore was called *Bou Thakuranir Haat*.

[153] Pratap Chandra Ghosh, *Bangadhip Parajay*, 2 volumes, 1869 and 1884, People's Press, Calcutta. This book also provided the material for Tagore's *Bou Thakuranir Haat*.

the other by Ahalya Bai. Ahalya Bai's public works in Benaras included the reconstruction of several temples,[154] the rehabilitation of various ghats and the building of dharamshalas. Rani Bhabani was also associated with several public works in the city. About Rani Bhabani, Manmatha Nath Dutt wrote, 'Temples with charity houses were built all over the country; countless tanks were dug to do away with the scarcity of water. In Benares she built many temples and established many charity-houses.' The factual basis for the Devi Chaudhuri story is very tenuous, though British records show that such a person did indeed exist. Therefore, Manmatha Nath Dutt essentially based his version on the Bankim Chandra Chatterji novel.[155] This leaves Asamanya, Jagat Seth's daughter. While Jagat Seth was a familiar name, the name of his daughter was very unusual. That idea of Asamanya as a name probably came from a long-forgotten book, written by Upendra Kumara Ghosha in 1895.[156]

After so many years, *Gleanings from the Indian Classics*, Vol. II is still worth a read. What's also interesting about the book is the educated Bengali's take on the events of 1857. It wasn't as if Manmatha Nath Dutt was an exception. This was indeed the average educated Bengali's reaction. In the section on Rani of Jhansi, he writes:

> The whole of the memorable Mutiny has been disfigured by the most unprecedented cruelty and shedding of innocent blood. There could be no justification for the massacre of the English women and children. Never in the annals of India warriors were found to be so cowardly as to raise their swords upon helpless women and children. But the Mutiny was the work of low class ruffians who were picked up by the English Sergeants and enlisted as Sepoys. They had no sympathy of

[154] Kashi Vishwanath Temple was one of these.

[155] Bankim Chandra Chatterjee, *Devi Chaudhurani*, Bangiya Sahitya Parishad, 1884.

[156] Upendra Kumara Ghosha, *Asamanya, Daughter of Jagat Seth*, 1895.

> the members of the noble houses, and they kept themselves aloof from the Mutiny, or else India would have been lost to the English. We have searched through every page of the history of the Indian Mutiny, written both by friends and foes of the Indian people and we have not found any of them charging the Rani of Jhansi with the massacre of women and children. She never allowed her soldiers to participate in these bloody cruelties; she often tried to dissuade the Sepoys from the path of cowardice and ruffianism—and when she failed to turn them from cruelty and murder she separated herself from them and went away with her men to some other place.

Indeed, one of those pieces in *Gleanings from the Indian Classics*, Vol. II is about individuals who saved the English in the course of the mutiny.[157]

Gleanings from the Indian Classics, Vol. III had the secondary title, 'Prophets of Ind'. Published in 1899, it was considerably influenced by Swami Vivekananda. In the Introduction, Manmatha Nath Dutt writes:

> The Religion of the Hindus is not only the oldest religion of the world, but it is the most noble religion amongst all the religions of the civilized societies [...] It is not one religion, it is not one structure [...] It is like the palace, which if seen from a distance will appear to be but one stupendous building, but if examined closely, and if seen from the foot of its walls, it would appear to be a pile of buildings, one rising above the other.

The introduction to Volume III also had a longish quote from Swami Vivekananda's address at the Parliament of Religions in Chicago on 19 September 1893,[158] though, as I said earlier, it didn't mention

---

[157] This is a reference to 'A Group from the Past'.

[158] 'Paper on Hinduism', *Complete Works of Swami Vivekananda*, Vol. 1, Available at <https://en.wikisource.org/wiki/The_Complete_Works_of_Swami_Vivekananda/Volume_1/

Swami Vivekananda by name. Manmatha Nath Dutt went on to write in the introduction:

> The difficulty in understanding the religion of the Hindus is that it has three-fold aspects. All other religions have only one aspect, but Hinduism has three distinct features. These three might be termed the three great steps to attain salvation. The first is sacrifices, pujas etc. that is all that is done with the help of material objects. The second is mental culture, such as cultivating good qualities, subjugating bad passions and ennobling the mind in every way. The third is spiritual communion. The first two are denied by the other chief religions of the world, the last has mere a half-hearted support from them [...] In this little book we have attempted to place before our readers short biographies and the teachings of some of the great prophets of Hinduism.

Who were the prophets Manmatha Nath Dutt wrote about? Shri Krishna and Buddha, of course. The others, covered in less detail, were Sankara, Ramanuja, Ramanand and Kabir. Drawing on the Mahabharata, *Harivamsha*, *Bhagavata Purana* and Bhagavad Gita, the Krishna sketch was familiar territory. The Buddha sketch drew extensively on Rhys Davids.[159] It also mentioned the St Josaphat connection. 'Now who is this St Josaphat? The author, John of Damascus, said that the Saint was a son of an Indian king, but he became a hermit afterwards.'[160] He further added that he heard the story from men who came from India. 'It has now been proved beyond all doubt that Josaphat, which means *Budhisattva*, was no

---

Addresses_at_The_Parliament_of_Religions/Paper_on_Hinduism> (last accessed 2 January 2020).

[159] T.W. Rhys Davids, *Buddhism: Being A Sketch of the Life and Teachings of Gautama, the Buddha*, Society for Promoting Christian Knowledge, London, 1877.

[160] In the eighth century, St John of Damascus wrote a book titled *Life of Barlaam and Joaspah.*

other than Goutam Budha of *Kapilavastu*.' This was discussed in Rhys Davids and also figured in an earlier talk by Max Muller.[161] However, this interest in the Buddha led Manmatha Nath Dutt to write an extensive book on the Buddha, his life and his teachings in 1901. This drew quite extensively on Rhys Davids and Oldenberg's life of the Buddha.[162] But by bringing in a Hinduism perspective, Dutt imparted his own value addition. Nevertheless, today, there is not much in the Buddha book to trigger one's interest. One might as well read Oldenberg or Rhys Davids. There is also not much in the 1899 Ayurveda book as it was essentially based on a book by Thomas Wise.[163]

In the non-translation category, this leaves two other books. The first is the 1904 book on Hindu metaphysics. Unlike translations, or disseminating the works of others, this was Manmatha Nath Dutt's own take on what can loosely be called Moksha Dharma. He writes:

> While carrying on my studies in Hindu Philosophy, I felt the want of a handy volume in which a beginner, or one who has not had the time and opportunity of going through the numberless volumes in Sanskrit, dealing with this branch of Hindu literature, can find ready at hand a systematic exposition of the various important problems of Hindu Metaphysics [...] To remove the want, which at least I myself felt very much, I have gleaned these sheafs from my own field of labour with a view that they may be of some use to general readers and students of Hindu Philosophy [...] I have spared no pains and trouble to make this little treatise a preparatory ground for the study of higher subjects, and my labours will be amply rewarded

---

161 F. Max Müller, 'On the Migration of Fables', lecture delivered at the Royal Institution in 1870. Reprinted in *Chips from a German Workshop*, Charles Scribner's Sons, New York, 1881.

162 Hermann Oldenberg, *Buddha: His Life, His Doctrine, His Order* (translated by William Hoey), Williams and Norgate, London, 1882.

163 Thomas Wise, *Review of the History of Medicine*, J. Churchill, London, 1867.

> if, by the perusal of my humble work, one single reader finds himself interested in the study of Hindu Metaphysics.

Unlike the other Manmatha Nath Dutt books, this was replete with quotes in Sanskrit, given as footnotes, from the Upanishads, the Bhagavad Gita, the *Yoga Vasishtha Ramayana*, the *Bhagavata Purana* and even tantra texts.[164] As mentioned earlier, even when he was quoted, Swami Vivekananda was not referred to by name. This is the first book where Manmatha Nath Dutt mentioned Shri Ramakrishna by name and quoted him. The quote was from what came to be known as *Kathamrita* in Bengali and *The Gospel of Sri Ramakrishna* in the English translation, based on a diary maintained by a disciple named Mahendra Nath Gupta, more commonly known as 'M'. The Bengali versions, in five volumes, were published between 1902 and 1932. The English version that is often read now is a 1942 translation, done by Swami Nikhilananda. M published a few pages of the diary in Bengali, in the form of a pamphlet. This led to a letter of encouragement from Swami Vivekananda. Thereafter, from October 1897, in a magazine known as *Brahmavadin*, M serialized the diary under the title *Leaves from the Gospel of the Lord Sri Ramakrishna*. This was a version in English and this was the source Manmatha Nath Dutt quoted from. It is a version that is now difficult to get. Today, there are several books on the gist of Moksha Dharma. Nevertheless, his book on Hindu metaphyisics stands the test of time. His language was never archaic and doesn't feel archaic, even today.

The 1905 book on domestic duty was even more remarkable. After all, Hinduism is often equated with the pursuit of moksha, and it is the corresponding texts that are invariably quoted. However, most people are in the *garhasthya* or householder stage, not in *vanaprastha* or *sanyasa*. But, rarely do they find a mention.

---

[164] A piece on *maya* by Nandalal Dhole was also inserted, indicating that, even in 1904, Manmatha Nath Dutt was in touch with Heeralal Dhole, whose permission was required.

> The life of a householder is the training ground for the acquisition of a higher life [...] I have attempted to collect in this small work, the various sacred injunctions of the Rishis about personal duties and responsibilities, and I shall consider my labours amply rewarded, if, by the perusal of these pages, even one of my countrymen becomes an ideal Hindu.

Being an ideal Hindu never meant the avoidance of the pursuits of *kama* and *artha*. Since this was written in 1905, the following quotes are quite remarkable.

> The degeneration and poverty of the present day Hindus is mainly due to their apathy for commercial and agricultural undertakings and hankering after service for making money. Even some of them foolishly believe that respectability lies in holding a Government appointment, and not in the pursuit of trade, for they do not know that a humble trader is thousand-fold happier than they, for he enjoys the sweets of independence. Therefore to those of our readers, who wish to earn money, we beg to suggest that they must take to commerce and agriculture, trade and manufacture and not to service.

This could only have been written by someone with a trace of entrepreneurship. He further writes:

> The greatest defect in our Indian character is that we start business without having received any education in the line. The common thing in India is that a journalist, carrying considerable influence with the public or enjoying a wide-spread reputation, floats a joint-stock company for carrying on a business of which he is quite ignorant. He becomes the Director of the same business without having any previous training in it. Again we find a millionaire starting a new business, having no practical knowledge of the same [...] Our rich people, if they wish to set their sons in business, should first of all qualify them for

> any particular line of work they may happen to chose [*sic*], by placing them under the tuition of experts.

These aren't statements one normally associates with a translator. I do not think Kisari Mohan Ganguli would have made either of those statements. But, as I have explained, Manmatha Nath Dutt's background was different.

EPILOGUE

Clearly, as a translator, and as a non-translator author, Manmatha Nath Dutt should have been remembered much more. Why isn't he? There are several strands in the answer and there is no uni-causal explanation, with all these different strands in the anwers impinging on each other.

First, that was a different day and age. People were less concerned about 'I' and 'mine'. Ganguli and Dutt worked on their translations as labours of love, though Manmatha Nath Dutt was also a bookseller and publisher. They were less concerned about recognition. Consequently, the Ganguli translation was known for a long time as the P.C. Roy translation and it was P.C. Roy who got the Commander of Indian Empire (CIE), though Ganguli eventually got a pension. The Manmatha Nath Dutt translations and other books were known to be his work, but beyond that, there were no biographies on dust jackets telling us about him. The age of marketing hadn't yet arrived; at least not in the sense we understand it today. Manmatha Nath Dutt was MA MRAS, Rector (Keshub Academy) and 'Shastri'. No other information was volunteered and no other information remained for posterity.

Second, Ganguli had a publisher who took care of marketing, distribution and publicity. All of Manmatha Nath Dutt's books were self-publishing initiatives. Self-publishing then, and the principles are no different today, had pros, but it also had cons. Once Manmatha Nath Dutt died in 1912, everything just fell apart—the society wound up, Elysium Press vanished and *The Wealth of India* ceased publication. There was no one left to carry anything forward. The managing agent evidently didn't do much. In today's jargon, there was no succession planning for the society, for Elysium Press, or for *The Wealth of India* and the books. But even more importantly, there was a trade-off between Manmatha Nath Dutt's objectives as a translator and Manmatha Nath Dutt's objectives as a bookseller cum publisher. In this trade-off, the translator objective suffered. The quality of translation suffered. The perception about quality suffered. Finally, the perception about Manmatha Nath Dutt himself suffered, with him being increasingly described as a bookseller and a publisher. As a publisher trying to sell his books, Manmatha Nath Dutt also contributed to this dilution, by rehashing the translations of Ganguli, Pargiter and Wilson, instead of focusing on his own translations. The Valmiki Ramayana translation, or that of the *Garuda Purana*, or the Dharmashastra texts, show that Manmatha Nath Dutt was perfectly capable of such independent translations. He did not need to borrow from the works of other authors. He did that because of his interests as a publisher, and in the process he not only diluted the quality of the translation, but also the production quality. He delegated the translation work to others and the quality of supervision left a lot to be desired.

Third, the legacy is often carried forward by descendants. The memories are carried forward by descendants. Family trees are reconstructed by descendants. In Manmatha Nath Dutt's case, the wife, Charubala, died around 1891. We don't know for sure that he married a second time. He probably did not. The daughter, Prembala, and the two sons, were brought up by the in-laws. Prembala lived in distant Ambala. At least one of the sons went off to Kuala Lumpur. We don't know what happened to the second son. Sucheta Kriplani does suggest that these two sons maintained distant relationships with the rest of the family with an emphasis on the adjective 'distant'. The daughter and sons did not seem to have had any links with Manmatha Nath Dutt after their mother died. There was a distancing there too. Hence, their ties with him were at best tenuous and they weren't interested in his memory or legacy. Years down the line, if he was at all remembered, it was by non-family members such as Sanat K. Roy Chowdhury. Add to that a speculative hypothesis. In 1912, when he died, Manmatha Nath Dutt wasn't an unknown name, as an author or translator. The newspapers and magazines of the day didn't carry obituaries like they do now, at least not for non-Europeans. Nevertheless, the news of his death should have appeared as a news item, even if not as an obituary. But there seems to have been nothing. Hence, it is possible that he didn't die in Calcutta. Having died elsewhere, his death too went unnoticed. If he wasn't from the Hatkhola lineage, but from what is now Bangladesh, and we have established that this was indeed the case, his parents and other family members would have been there and not in Calcutta. Also, due to his having become a Brahmo, his parents had probably disowned him. His mother had probably died in his childhood. The family there had no reason to remember him and there was no family in Calcutta to remember him. Did he die on a visit to wherever his ancestral roots happened to be, in Sagarkandi, or elsewhere in Pabna? Did he die on a visit to Varanasi? Was that why there was no news item? No one knew about his death and no one cared about Babu Manmatha Nath Dutt.

Fourth, Manmatha Nath Dutt didn't live that long. With some marginal differences between males and females, in 1901, the life expectancy at birth was 24 years in India. Therefore, a statement about Manmatha Nath Dutt not living long enough needs qualification. He did live for 47 years and that is not insignificant. At the time, 24 was the average life expectancy and it was low because of a variety of health-related factors, but it wasn't the life expectancy across all classes. To state it differently, if one survives till a certain age, the life expectancy increases. This comes across in what demographers call life-tables, not life expectancy at birth, but life expectancy at various ages. For example, in one such reconstructed life-table for India in 1901, if a male survived till the age of 50, his life expectancy was actually 68.67 years.[165] Rabindranath Tagore lived till the age of 80, Sivanath Sastri till the age of 72, Romesh Chunder Dutt till the age of 61, Hirendranath Dutta till the age of 72 and so on. Compared to his contemporaries, who belonged to the same class of society, Manmatha Nath Dutt didn't live that long.

Fifth, fame is often not only a function of what one does individually, but also of the collective entity to which one belongs. Manmatha Nath Dutt was never identified with any of the religious movements of the time—Christianity, the theosophist movement, the Brahmo Samaj, the Ramakrishna Mission. He had friends who were theosophists, but he wasn't one. He had friends who were Brahmos, and so probably was he, but he was never intimately associated with any of the Brahmo Samaj activities. After the schism within the Brahmo Samaj, he identified with the less influential wing. And despite being a Brahmo, particularly after Swami Vivekananda in Chicago, he was increasingly attracted towards Hinduism. To state it more bluntly, his religious beliefs were somewhat ambivalent and confused and would probably have evolved and crystallized more had he lived longer. But as things stood, he was not a member of any of the collective religious movements and lacked that identity. To compound matters, he didn't get identified with the nationalist movement either, not even with the 1905 Partition of Bengal, which had Bengal in a tumult. The nationalist movement, or the 1905 Partition, finds no mention in anything that he wrote. If anything, despite the obvious pride in the Hindu heritage, his general tone was that of currying favour with the current colonial government.

---

[165] Bagsmrita Bhagawati and Labananda Choudhury, 'Generation Life Table for India, 1901-1951', *Middle East Journal of Age and Ageing,* Vol. 12, Issue 3, October 2015.

Was that because his father and uncle had made their fortune as contractors with the railways? Therefore, he lacked that collective identity too. Whatever he pursued was his individual search for the truth, as he perceived it. Consequently, there was never a collective body that would carry his legacy and memory forward.

Sixth, he never quite overcame that branding of a dilettante, not a professional. In the area of translations and editions of ancient texts, Bengal was an amazing reservoir of talent then. Kaliprasanna Singha (1841–1870) translated the entire unabridged Mahabharata into Bengali. Between 1862 and 1873, the Burdwan edition of the Mahabharata was brought out, in Sanskrit, and with a Bengali translation. I have already mentioned the Bengali translation brought out between 1869 and 1874 by Pratap Chandra Roy. William Carey and Joshua Marshman brought out an English translation of Valmiki Ramayana between 1806 and 1810, from Serampore. More or less at the same time, Hemachandra Bhattacharya brought out a translation in Bengali. Ganga Prasad Mukhopadhyaya, Ashutosh Mukherjee's father, did a translation of the Valmiki Ramayana in Bengali, in verse form. Panchanan Tarkaratna (1866–1940), whose background as a traditional Sanskrit scholar from Bhatpara was the polar opposite of Manmatha Nath Dutt's, edited many Sanskrit texts and translated them into Bengali. This included Valmiki Ramayana, Adhyatma Ramayana, Dharmashastra texts and several Puranas. Michael Madhusudan Dutt (1824–1873) did his version of the Ramayana story, *Meghnad Badh Kavya* (The Slaying of Meghnada). There were also the Bibliotheca Indica editions. In 1840, Horace Hayman Wilson (1786–1860) published the first unabridged English translation of any Purana, the *Vishnu Purana*. Hara Prasad Shastri (1853–1931) was busy collecting manuscripts from Nepal and translating the Buddhist Puranas. As in other areas of intellectual activity, there was a surfeit of talent in Sanskrit scholarship too. Manmatha Nath Dutt's contribution never quite registered in the general consciousness. As we have seen, his 'Shastri' degree was probably honorary and he never obtained the respect of proper scholars. He fell between the two stools of the popular and the academically proper. A bookseller and publisher, not even a translator, dabbling in such matters. While this wasn't entirely true, but it may well have been the perception. However, we should no longer have that perception. Without a doubt, he was a most extraordinary translator and author, who would probably have been better off had he stuck to Deva Press and not become an entrepreneur, starting his own Elysium Press.

ACKNOWLEDGEMENTS

This book, about the great translator Manmatha Nath Dutt, is an unusual one on a very unusual subject. In gathering the material for this book, there were several people who have at different stages contributed by providing help and small bits of information. I have a special debt to Arun Chakraborty (Former Director-General, National Library, Kolkata), Jayaprabha Ravindran (Assistant Director, National Archives of India), Kumar Sanjay (Chief Librarian, NITI Aayog), Laveesh Bhandari (Director, Indicus), Makarand Paranjape (Director, Indian Institute of Advanced Study, Shimla), Maurice Klapwald (Assistant Manager, The New York Public Library), Meghna Sharma, P.V. Ramesh (Former Director-General, National Archives of India), Partha Sarathi Das (ALIO, National Library, Kolkata), S. Prasannarajan (Editor, *Open* magazine), Sanatan Ghosh (Deputy Director, Government of West Bengal), Sandeep Chakravorty (Consul General of India, New York), Sanjeev Sanyal (Principal Economic Adviser, Ministry of Finance), Shakti Sinha (Former Director, Nehru Memorial Museum and Library) and Shashi Sekhar (CEO, Prasar Bharati). *Open* magazine carried a few early essays on Manmatha Nath Dutt and I wish to thank several readers for their comments, persuading me that this subject was worthy of a book. A book on such an unusual subject might never have materialized had it not been for the great team at Rupa

Publications, who were very forthcoming in welcoming the idea.

This is by no means a biography of Manmatha Nath Dutt, because there are still many gaps in the account. For example, I have still not been able to ascertain where he died in 1912. I have not been able to conclusively establish that the title of 'Shastri' was conferred on him by the then Maharaja of Mysore. Though my suspicion is that this is what happened, I have not included it in the text because I have no firm basis for this speculation. Nor do I have any firm evidence for my hunch that he was drawn towards the Theosophcial Society because of the influence of Parbati Churn Roy, Prasanna Kumar Sen's maternal uncle. Since so little is known about him, I hope this book will only be a trigger for historians and researchers to flesh out a more complete biography.

Bibek Debroy
January 2020

www.ingramcontent.com/pod-product-compliance
Lightning Source LLC
Chambersburg PA
CBHW010757310726
48980CB00009B/819/J

* 9 7 8 9 3 8 9 9 6 7 0 1 2 *